TAMING MR. WILDER

THE BILLIONAIRE HEARTS CLUB

KELLY COLLINS

Prologue
THE OATH

Harvard University, September 15, 2009

We, Ronan Wilder, Knox Knightly, and Gabriel Sterling, do hereby establish **THE OATH.**

RECOGNIZING: *That monumental careers await, and that premature personal commitments will only hinder our rise to success.*

WE THEREFORE PLEDGE:
Clause I: Freedom Until Forty. We vow to remain unencumbered by matrimony, focusing solely on our ambitions until we each attain the age of forty (40). Professional pursuits shall be paramount; significant personal entanglements are deferred.

Clause II: The Binding Nature of This Oath. This Oath is declared with full seriousness. There shall be no withdrawals or justifications for breach.

Clause III: Ramifications of Breach. Should any signatory violate this sacred pledge, the following penalties will be enforced: a. The offending party must furnish a lavish and diverse supply of premium alcoholic beverages—essentially, the means for a legendary, fully stocked bar—to be divided amongst the loyal signatories. b.

Furthermore, he shall endure a minimum of one decade of spirited and imaginative ridicule from the remaining members.

Affirmed and signed on this date,

Ronan Wilder

Knox Knightly

Gabriel Sterling

Chapter 1

RONAN WILDER DIDN'T SIT in his leather chair—he possessed it. From his perch on the fortieth floor of Oath Capital, he presided over a kingdom of glass and steel, the expansive conference table before him a battlefield where projections bled and profits were slain. Outside, the city hummed, a distant, muted thing, background noise to the symphony of commerce he conducted. Inside, the air was his—still, cold, and tense with the silent, brutal weight of numbers.

A crisp blue graph illuminated the wall-mounted screen, the upward trend an objective, satisfying fact. Knox Knightly, his CFO and oldest friend, was the picture of meticulous precision in a gray three-piece suit that mirrored the city below. He adjusted his glasses, his reflection a faint ghost in the polished table.

"Revenue is up seven percent this quarter," Knox stated, his tone clipped and devoid of celebration. It was merely a fact, a starting point for the next assault. "But we'll need to tighten operational costs to maintain that margin going into Q3." He glanced at the third man at the table. Where Knox was caution, Gabriel Sterling was pure velocity, a man who saw every conversation as an angle to be played.

"Already streamlined." Gabriel leaned forward, his signature confidence radiating from a perpetually loosened tie and the sharp-edged energy of a man who thrived on disruption. "I've got the team restructuring vendor contracts. We'll shave two percent off by next month."

"Good." Ronan's voice cut through the air, a blade of ice. He tapped the edge of his tablet, new projections scrolling beneath his thumb. His features were a mask of neutrality, a carefully constructed facade that betrayed nothing. "But not good enough. I want four percent. Half-measures are a waste of resources."

Knox and Gabriel exchanged a look, a silent, two-second negotiation he'd learned to ignore on principle. He knew what they were thinking. It was an aggressive, perhaps impossible target. But impossible targets were the only ones worth aiming for. They were the building blocks of empires. Let them worry about his standards. He didn't lower them for market fluctuations, for competitors, and certainly not for the comfort of his own partners. He was the engine, and his expectations were the fuel.

"Four percent it is," Gabriel said finally, a challenge glinting in his eyes. He lived for the impossible number. Knox gave a subtle, resigned nod.

"Meeting adjourned." Ronan's attention was already back on his glowing screen, the men dissolving from his focus as he immersed himself in a fresh set of analytics. "Knox, have the updated numbers on my desk by end of day. Gabriel, ensure procurement understands what's at stake. No excuses."

The men gathered their laptops without argument. The atmosphere he cultivated was one of ruthless efficiency, where decisions were swift and emotion was a liability left at the door. He'd built his life on that principle, constructing a fortress of logic and control where nothing could touch him. It was how he liked it, clean and predictable.

He had exactly eight seconds of the order he craved before his world was invaded.

"Knock, knock!"

The cheerful interruption came from the doorway, a sound as out of place as a songbird in a morgue. The scent of fresh coffee and something else—citrus and pear, bright and defiant—cut through the sterile, filtered air of his office. Devney Sinclair, his assistant and the sole unpredictable variable in his life, entered. She balanced a cup of coffee in one hand, her bright yellow blouse an assault of sun against the office's muted tones of charcoal and chrome. Her grin was blinding, wide and utterly unbothered by his perpetual scowl.

"Your coffee," she announced, placing a steaming cup on his desk with a flourish. "Two hundred two degrees. Because you're a menace to society without it. You're welcome."

His eyes remained locked on the tablet, the numbers a familiar, grounding anchor. "Leave it on the desk, Devney."

"Can do," she chirped. He heard the soft click of the ceramic against the glass.

The deliberate scrape of a chair being pulled forward made Ronan's head snapped up. She sat, crossing her legs, an infuriatingly pleasant smile fixed on her face as if she'd been invited. She was the only person at Oath Capital who dared.

"While I have you," she began, "a small detail about the upcoming charity gala."

His silent look didn't intimidate her.

"You should go."

"Pass." The word was an anvil dropped from a great height, a final, executive decision intended to end the conversation.

"You can't pass. It's not Blackjack." She leaned forward, resting her elbows on his desk, invading his carefully defined personal space. "It's an excellent networking opportunity. I confirmed Andrew Beauchamp will be there—just like I promised. You've been trying to get a meeting with him for months."

That gave him pause. Beauchamp was old money, a titan of industry with a portfolio that could secure Oath Capital's dominance for the next decade. He was also notoriously traditional, valuing face-to-face interactions over cold calls. A gala was exactly the sort of venue Beauchamp favored. Devney, of course, would know that. She knew his own schedule and his targets better than he did sometimes.

"I'll schedule a proper meeting with Beauchamp. One that doesn't involve string quartets and overpriced gift baskets filled with artisanal jams."

"What do you have against artisanal jams?" she asked, her expression one of mock horror. "Besides, this isn't about jams. This is about showing a human side. Think of it as exposure therapy."

He finally granted her his full attention, his gaze cold enough to freeze assets. "For what? My aversion to wasting time?"

"Your allergy to fun," she countered, her eyes alight with the thrill of debate. "It's a serious condition. Symptoms include a chronic inability to mingle, an irrational fear of cocktail hour, and the core belief that joy is an inefficient allocation of emotional resources."

"Sinclair," he started, the warning in his voice low and clear. He should fire her. The thought was a common one. He could have any assistant in the city, someone quiet, efficient, someone who wouldn't fill his office with bright colors and persistently cheerful banter. Someone who wouldn't challenge him.

But the silence in this office when she wasn't here was absolute, and lately it had started to feel less like peace and more like absence.

"You're one step away from becoming a full-fledged robot, Ronan," she pressed on, undeterred, leaning so close he could see the tiny flecks of green in her hazel eyes. "This is my intervention. Before you start trying to schedule joy into fifteen-minute increments on your calendar."

He leaned back in his chair, the leather groaning in protest. He steepled his fingers, regarding her as he would a hostile variable in a market projection. "My idea of fun," he stated, his voice flat, "is closing a deal that adds seven figures to our quarterly revenue."

"Wow," she blinked. "You know how to party. But what's the point of conquering Wall Street," she asked, with a tone that was warmer, more persuasive, "if you can't pause to enjoy an absurdly small egg tart?"

He stared at her, momentarily thrown by the sheer, infuriating illogicality of the statement. Mini quiches. That was her argument. An argument about appetizers was somehow meant to dismantle a life philosophy he'd spent two decades building. A philosophy born from watching his parents use cocktail parties as battlegrounds, their smiles as weapons, their laughter sharp-edged and cruel. He avoided such events not because he disliked them but because he understood them all too well. They were arenas of insincerity and emotional carnage.

He dragged a hand down his face, the carefully constructed walls of his composure beginning to crumble under the relentless assault of her cheerfulness. She wasn't just chipping away at his defenses, she was taking a brightly colored sledgehammer to them, and he was growing tired of rebuilding them every time she left his office.

"Fine," he grated out, the word tasting like defeat, like swallowing gravel. "I'll consider it."

"Excellent!" She stood in a single fluid motion, brushing an imaginary wrinkle from her skirt. Her victory was quiet but absolute. "Small victories." She turned for the door, then paused, a glint of pure, unadulterated mischief in her eyes. "Oh, and for your consideration? I've already RSVP'd for two."

She disappeared into the hallway, leaving him staring at the empty doorway. The scent of her perfume, that defiant splash of citrus and pear, lingered in the air, a contaminant in his sterile world. His inbox was full. His schedule was packed. He had an empire to run.

And yet, as he reached for the coffee cup, its warmth seeping into his hand, her RSVP was the loudest thing in the room.

Chapter 2

DEVNEY SKIPPED BACK to her desk and dropped into her chair with a little bounce, a triumphant grin plastered across her face. Her insistent push in Ronan's office had finally done the trick.

She could still hear his gruff "Fine, I'll consider it ringing in her ears. It was a reply she had wrangled out of him after twenty minutes of relentless charm, persuasion, and maybe a teensy bit of manipulation.

"Take that, Mr. Doom-and-Gloom," she whispered under her breath, jotting down "Gala: Confirmed" with a flourish. If the universe kept score of her wins against him, she'd earned herself a gold star.

The office around her hummed with its usual intensity. Keyboards clicked, and phones rang at exact intervals. The space was a temple to order and control, with glass partitions, spotless desks aligned at perfect ninety-degree angles, even the air smelled faintly of expensive leather and fresh paper.

Her desk was chaos, a rebellion of color in a kingdom of straight lines. A potted succulent wearing a tiny sombrero sat by her computer. A stack of pastel sticky notes teetered precariously, and nestled among her pens was a bedazzled sunflower pen she reserved for moments when she wanted to annoy her boss.

Julia from Accounting peeked over her monitor with a raised brow and a smirk

"Mission accomplished." Devney twisted in her chair. "Ronan Wilder is officially going to the gala."

Julia's eyes widened. "You convinced him? To attend a social event? Does he know there's mingling involved?"

"Don't remind me," Devney laughed. "I had to promise him it wasn't technically small talk if it was business-related."

"Impressive. You deserve a medal, or hazard pay."

"Doing my part to keep things interesting around here." She winked before turning back to her computer.

Around her, heads popped up from cubicles, eyebrows lifting, glances shifting. Devney, in high spirits, had a ripple effect. Her energy lessened the starch in the air, loosening ties and coaxing the corners of mouths upward. Even the eternally grim IT guy looked marginally less haunted whenever she passed by him.

"Sinclair," a familiar, deep voice cut sharply from behind her.

She didn't jump. Months of working under him had taught her to expect his stealthy approach.

"Yes, Mr. Wilder?" she responded sweetly, spinning her chair halfway to look up at him. He loomed in her peripheral vision, tall and sharp like a perfectly tailored storm cloud.

"Did you confirm the caterer for next week's board meeting?" he asked.

"Done and dusted yesterday," she said. "Menu finalized, including vegan options because apparently Mr. Hargrove has opinions about cheese."

"Good," he clipped out, but his eyes lingered a fraction

longer than necessary before he turned and strode back into his office.

She pressed her lips together, barely suppressing her satisfaction as she watched him retreat. Now she could officially add "getting Ronan Wilder to a gala" to her list of unlikely victories.

Team Sunshine: one. Grumpy CEO: zero.

"Step one, Operation Loosen-Up-Ronan, is officially underway," she muttered under her breath.

The man needed a crash course in joy. A little laughter. A little lightness. Maybe even, dare she dream, happiness.

Her eyes drifted to her computer screen. The Amazon tab was already open. If anyone could dismantle Ronan Wilder's precisely built defenses, it was Devney Sinclair—and possibly the power of absurdly funny books.

She added several titles to her cart: *How to Chill: A Guide for the Perpetually Uptight*, *How to Appear Normal at Social Events*, and her favorite discovery, *Unicorns Are Jerks*: A Coloring Book Exposing Their Fluffy Underbellies. She snorted, already picturing his expression when he saw that one.

"Baby steps, Sinclair," she coached herself, as she completed her purchase. "Getting Ronan Wilder to look remotely pleased is definitely a multi-day project."

When the delivery man arrived from Sal's Deli, she collected Ronan's lunch and carried it to his office, knocking on the frame before stepping inside.

"Your lunch is here," she announced, holding up the bag.

As expected, he didn't look up, deep in a spreadsheet or quarterly analysis.

"Noted," he responded quietly, still not glancing her way.

She unpacked his sandwich and set his smoothie down with a thud. "Turkey club, extra avocado, no onion, sourdough bread, light mayo. And yes, I remembered the spinach smoothie with flaxseed and absolutely no banana, because apparently bananas are the devil's fruit."

That made him pause. His eyes lifted, sharp and assessing. "How do you keep track of all this?" he wondered.

"Because, Mr. Wilder," her voice dipped into mock gravity, "I am good at my job."

"Impressive," he acknowledged quietly, finally reaching for the smoothie like a man accepting a reluctant truce.

By the end of the day, her Amazon package had arrived. She carried the box to his office and set it squarely in the middle of his desk with a victorious flourish.

"What's this?" he questioned, eyeing the plain cardboard box warily.

"An essential addition to your personal library." She folded her arms. "Trust me, you'll thank me later."

He sliced the tape open, pulling out each book with growing disbelief. When he reached *Unicorns Are Jerks*, he stared at the cover for a long moment.

"Unicorns," he stated flatly.

"Jerks," she confirmed, nodding.

With a sigh, he closed the box and folded his hands on top of it. "You're aware that I run a multibillion-dollar investment firm, correct?"

"Mm-hmm." She rocked back on her heels, her grin unfaltering. "And you're welcome."

His lips pressed into a thin line, though the edge wavered like he was fighting off a laugh.

"Fine. But don't expect me to color any unicorns."

She backed toward the door. "Rome wasn't built in a day."

"Neither was my patience," he muttered, but she caught it —and the faintest lift at the corner of his mouth.

"Goodnight, Ronan."

"Goodnight, Devney." His tone was so muted she wondered if he'd spoken at all.

THE BAR WAS INVITING as she stepped inside, spotting Lucy at a high-top table near the window, already halfway through what looked like a generous pour of Merlot. Her friend had closed Flour & Honey early to meet her—a rare occurrence for someone who lived and breathed her Park Slope bakery.

"Finally!" Lucy exclaimed. "I was thinking you and your grumpy billionaire got caught up solving a corporate crisis or eloping to Fiji."

"Ha, ha." Devney slid onto the stool across from her friend. "For the record, Ronan would never go to Fiji. That would give in to fun. And no crises today, only me saving the world one sandwich order at a time."

"Heroic," Lucy acknowledged, raising her glass in a salute.

After ordering her wine, Devney leaned in conspiratorially. "Okay, so, you are going to love this."

"Out with it," Lucy urged. "You're wearing the grin of a child who's unearthed the hidden cookie jar."

"I got him to agree to go to a gala."

Lucy blinked. Then blinked again. "Wait, what? Your boss is willingly attending a social function that isn't a power lunch? You're joking."

"Scout's honor." Devney held up three fingers. "And it wasn't even that hard! A little charm, a lot of persistence, and maybe the tiniest bit of emotional manipulation."

"Unbelievable," Lucy breathed, shaking her head with a grin. "You must have some kind of superpower."

"I think our frosty CEO is thawing a tad," Devney mused. "We're making headway one painstakingly precise sugar grain at a time."

"Or maybe he's realized how charming you are and can't say no to that sunshiny face of yours."

"Doubtful," Devney laughed, though her cheeks heated.

"He probably figured it was easier to give in than listen to me nag him about it for another week."

Lucy went still for a beat. "You sure there's not more going on here? Like maybe you're trying to get him out of his fortress of solitude because you actually care if he has fun?"

"Of course I care," Devney admitted. "I mean, it's my job to make sure he shows up to these things and doesn't look like he'd rather be doing long division in his office."

"Mm-hmm," Lucy hummed, clearly unconvinced. "And that's all it is? Professional concern?"

"Yes," Devney insisted, though she couldn't ignore the way Lucy's smug little grin made her stomach do a weird little flip.

"People aren't résumés, Dev," Lucy pointed out, leaning forward. "And for the record, I've seen you blush twice since we started talking about him."

"That's because you're embarrassing me!" Devney protested. "Seriously, there's nothing there. He's my boss, and we could not be more different if we tried. Oil and water, remember?"

"But you know what they say about opposites attracting…"

"Lucy!"

"Okay, okay, I'll stop. For now." Lucy raised her glass with a wink. "But mark my words, this is not the last time we're having this conversation."

As they continued sipping their drinks, Lucy leaned forward, her eyes lit up with the kind of gleam that promised chaos and cocktails. "So, when he agreed to go to this oh-so-important gala, it wasn't because you batted those Bambi eyes of yours and he melted like a forgotten ice cream cone?"

Devney nearly choked on her laugh. "I don't bat my eyes!"

"You hesitated." Lucy leaned forward with a wicked grin. "You totally hesitated."

"That proves nothing," Devney shot back, but her cheeks betrayed her, heating despite her best efforts.

"For someone who claims there's 'nothing there,' you sure get pink whenever his name comes up."

Devney groaned. "Stop," she begged, covering her face with both hands. "Seriously, Lucy, this is ridiculous. He's my boss. My grumpy boss. End of story. There's no attraction or whatever you're trying to imply."

"Sure, sure," Lucy conceded, nodding. "No attraction whatsoever. That's why you spend half your day trying to get a reaction out of him, and the other half pretending you don't notice how annoyingly good he looks."

"Lucy Wang, I swear to all things holy—"

"Relax, Dev. Your secret's safe with me. For now." Lucy's tone was light. Then, with a sly grin, she added, "But seriously, have you considered that your little 'mission' to loosen him up might be step one in your grand plan to become Mrs. Wilder?"

Devney's jaw dropped. "Excuse me?"

"All I'm saying is," Lucy continued, "I've heard the way you talk about him. You two already have this spark. It's practically a fire hazard. Throw in this gala event, and who can predict what might happen."

"You are officially the worst."

"Maybe. But I'm also right. And when you two inevitably end up together, I expect full credit as your fairy godfriend."

"Not happening," Devney stated firmly, though the heat in her cheeks made her doubt her own words.

"Whatever you say, Dev, but don't think for a second that I'm letting this go."

Lucy raised her glass. "To you, Devs. For surviving another day in the trenches of corporate America and somehow staying your ridiculously optimistic self."

"To us," Devney echoed, tapping her glass against Lucy's. "For always having each other's backs and calling out nonsense at exactly the right moment."

As they sipped their drinks, she felt a warm glow settle over her. No matter how chaotic or confusing her life became, whether it involved grumpy billionaires or gala planning, she knew she could face it all. With Lucy in her corner and her own unshakable optimism, anything seemed possible. Even maybe figuring out the mystery that was Ronan Wilder.

Chapter 3

THE DOORMAN GREETED him with a polite nod, and he returned it with the faintest of gestures, his dark hair slicked back and not a wrinkle or stray thread in sight on his tailored suit. He adjusted his tie as he pushed through the heavy glass doors. The scent of butter and sage greeted him as he stepped inside—elegant, expensive, a little too strong. The restaurant buzzed, muted conversations layered over the clink of silverware and the delicate strains of piano music, peppered by bursts of laughter.

His polished shoes tapped against the marble floor as he strode forward, every movement purposeful.

Heads turned, not because he demanded attention, but because he had it. A waiter made the mistake of hovering too long in his path; one arched brow from Ronan sent the poor man scurrying away like a startled rabbit.

Gabriel was mid-conversation, one hand moving with restrained precision, the other hovering near his wine glass—every motion intentional, like everything else he did.

Knox, broad-shouldered and grinning like he'd pulled off a

heist, leaned back with the confidence of someone who didn't mind being the loudest man in the room.

"Well, well." Knox's voice carried enough volume to make two nearby tables glance their way as Ronan approached. "Look who's graced us with his presence. Did you take a meeting on the way here…or did your GPS just figure out how to get across town?"

"Knox." Ronan's voice was even. "Still finding new ways to test my patience."

Their usual firm handshake morphed into a fleeting, hearty pat on the back, a show of brotherhood that Knox wouldn't even dream of initiating within the sleek confines of their office. There, the demarcation line between friendship and commerce was rigidly enforced.

"Good to see you." Gabriel rose next, extending a hand. His grip was solid, his green eyes crinkling with genuine affection. "We were thinking you'd been kidnapped by your inbox again."

"Only a near miss," Ronan replied, the corners of his mouth shifting enough to suggest he wasn't entirely unimpressed. This was as close as he got to looking remotely pleased without a multimillion-dollar deal on the table.

Their server arrived, notepad in hand, and the ordering proceeded with ease: a medium rare ribeye for Knox, grilled salmon for Ronan, and the predictable roasted chicken for Gabriel.

Ronan's eyes scanned the wine selection, then set down the list and looked at the bottle open on the table—an expensive cabernet. "Judging by this choice, it seems neither of you deemed me fit to be part of tonight's decision."

"That's because you're set in your ways." Knox reached for the bottle and poured Ronan a glass before he could protest. "You'd have picked a vintage so painfully dull, our poor server would've nodded off while uncorking the bottle."

"Dull?" Ronan challenged. "Big words coming from someone who's never strayed from roasted chicken on a menu."

"Why tamper with what works?" Gabriel returned, with a grin that reached his eyes, hoisting his wine glass for their traditional toast.

"Could we perhaps hold off on the banter?" Knox interjected, more amused than annoyed. "Some of us like to ease into a peaceful dinner."

Gabriel leaned back. "Same table, same chaos." Their corner booth in the private dining room had become a ritual—monthly dinners where business mixed with friendship, and the rest of the world stayed outside.

"Appreciated, Gabriel." Ronan reached for his glass and took a contemplative sip. He lifted it, studying the color. "At least someone remembers how to kick off a dinner properly."

"Proper," Knox scoffed, leaning forward with a smirk, "is overrated."

Gabriel studied him for a beat. "You look more serious than usual, and that's saying a lot."

Ronan lowered his glass, expression flat. "For good reason. There's a situation."

Gabriel exchanged a glance with Knox, his interest piqued. "What kind of situation?" he asked.

Ronan exhaled slowly. "Devney has taken her role as my personal assistant to a new level."

"How bad are we talking?" Gabriel asked.

"I've been lured into a charity ball."

Knox nearly choked on his wine in a burst of laughter

"Make sure you keep that invitation. Frame it. Let's showcase it in the office reception area under a plaque with her picture, reading 'Most Committed Employee.'"

Ronan shot him an unamused look before shifting restlessly in his chair. "Don't encourage her," he warned. "She also added a line item labeled 'emotional damages' to her expense report after I rejected her proposal for themed office snacks."

"Wait, hold on." Knox's expression caught somewhere between amusement and skepticism. "What exactly qualifies as 'themed' office snacks?"

"Apparently, matching the quarterly budget report to flavors of potato chips." Ronan didn't even blink. "Sour cream and onion for the losses, barbecue for gains."

Gabriel chuckled, shaking his head. "Sounds like she's keeping things lively."

"She's keeping things unhinged." Ronan leaned back as the waiter placed a fresh basket of bread on the table. He broke the bread in half, controlled even in irritation. "I can't decide if I should promote her for sheer audacity or fire her to protect my sanity."

"Promote her," Knox said. "Definitely promote her. If nothing else, it'll make your shareholder meetings wildly entertaining."

"Because that's what I need," Ronan countered, shaking his head. "More entertainment."

"Well, you can't fire her." Gabriel's tone was laced with that measured diplomacy he wielded so effortlessly. "She's clearly good at her job, even if she has unconventional methods. Besides, you'd miss her antics. Admit it."

"*Miss* is a strong word." The slight quirk of Ronan's lips suggested otherwise. "One doesn't miss earthquakes, tornados, and hurricanes."

A commotion on the far side of the restaurant drew their attention. A young man had dropped to one knee beside a candlelit table, producing a small velvet box that caught the light. The woman's hands flew to her mouth, tears already streaming down her face, as nearby diners turned to watch. Her emphatic nodding set off a round of applause, punctuated by the distinctive pop of a champagne cork.

Knox watched the scene unfold with an exaggerated grimace, as if he'd witnessed someone step in an unpleasant mess. "Speaking of natural disasters," he commented, leaning forward and resting his elbows on the polished mahogany table, "isn't it remarkable how we've upheld the pact?"

Ronan frowned. "The pact?"

"Don't feign ignorance, Wilder." Knox waved his fork in Ronan's direction. "You know exactly what I'm referring to. We remain free birds until we reach forty. No exceptions. No loopholes. And certainly, no bubbly assistants with glitter pens convincing you otherwise. Half of our old schoolmates are now sporting gold bands of servitude and dad bods while we're here enjoying our freedom."

"Ah, yes." Ronan's voice was flat. "How could I forget such a profoundly mature agreement?"

"Hey, it's called self-preservation," Knox defended. "We agreed. Careers first, complications later. We've made it this far—you're not bailing on us now."

"Trust me," Ronan assured him. "There's no risk of that."

"I'm making sure." Knox eased into a more relaxed position, a satisfied smirk playing on his lips. "You know I'm a stickler for the rules."

"That's hardly the term I'd use to describe you," Gabriel remarked, his tone light and edged with humor.

Knox shrugged nonchalantly, lifting his glass in a toast. "Label me as you wish. But a pact is a pact. Here's to remaining free and uncommitted."

Ronan and Gabriel raised their glasses, clinking them against Knox's. "Free, perhaps," Ronan murmured under his breath before taking a sip. "Uncommitted seems hopeful."

As if on cue, their server appeared at that moment, expertly balancing three plates of steaming entrees on his forearm. The tantalizing aroma of seared steak and roasted vegetables filled the air as he placed each dish before them.

"Perfect timing." Knox rubbed his hands together in anticipation as he eyed his ribeye. "I was about to start gnawing on the table."

"Your refined dining habits never cease to amaze." Ronan turned his attention to the seared salmon on his plate and reached for another slice of sourdough from the breadbasket.

"Some of us work up an appetite doing actual work," Knox said with a grin. "We can't all survive on spreadsheets and spite."

"Debatable on both counts," Ronan countered. The candlelight caught the rich burgundy of the wine in their glasses, casting ruby shadows across the crisp white tablecloth.

Ronan set his glass down. "Speaking of debates, there's a chance for me to meet with Andrew Beauchamp this weekend."

That name snapped Gabriel's attention from the breadbasket, while Knox set his glass down.

"Beauchamp," Knox drawled slowly. "The family-values kingpin himself. You're aiming high."

"Why wouldn't I?" Ronan said. "The man has a portfolio worth over six billion dollars. If we secure even a fraction of his interest—say, five hundred million—it would be a game changer for Oath Capital. We could expand into markets we've only dreamed about."

"Five hundred million?" Gabriel said with genuine interest. "What's your angle?"

"His record shows he values innovation paired with stability." Ronan's voice was low but even, as if he were outlining a battle plan. "He likes to see long-term growth potential backed by data. Our recent returns speak for themselves. Plus, Oath's diversification strategy aligns exactly with his investment philosophy."

"Impressive." Knox said. "But doesn't he also have eccentric preferences? Like, didn't he once reject a pitch because the CEO wore brown shoes to a meeting?"

"That was black shoes with navy socks," Gabriel corrected, chuckling. "Though your point still stands."

"Yes, well." Ronan brushed off the remark with a slight wave of his hand. "Eccentric or not, Beauchamp knows value when he sees it. And our numbers don't lie."

"True." Gabriel nodded. "Still, you know how he operates. The man likes to dig deeper than the spreadsheets. He'll want more than impressive charts."

"Which is why I'm prepared." Ronan shifted in his seat, the illusion of calm cracking. He should have felt relaxed—he was prepared—but the stiffness in his shoulders told a different story. "I've gone over every contingency, every possible objection he might raise. By the time this deal clears, he won't see Oath Capital as another run-of-the-mill firm. He'll see us as The Firm."

"Listen to you." Knox set down his fork. "The man sounds like he's already drafting the contract in his head."

"That's because I am," Ronan shot back. "This isn't some ordinary deal. This is leverage for the next ten years. It's influence. Security. It's—" He stopped himself, exhaling sharply. "It's everything."

"Everything, huh?" Knox swirled his drink. "No pressure, then."

"None whatsoever." Ronan's attention drifted to the candle at the center of the table. He watched its flame dance. Its erratic movement was an unwelcome echo of the way his own focus kept scattering.

Knox's tone was teasing as he gestured with his glass. "But there's one tiny detail you might want to iron out before you start ordering custom yachts." He paused, his expression turning serious. "Beauchamp's got a thing for investing in family men. Likes to see himself as a 'legacy builder,' or equally nauseating ideals. Word is, he prefers dealing with guys who have the whole white-picket-fence package—wife, kids, Golden Retriever, the works."

The words landed with a dull thud between them. Ronan's hand halted mid-reach for his drink—small, but telling, like someone had nudged his perfectly aligned chessboard. For half a beat, he remained still.

"Family men," he echoed flatly.

"Relax, Ronan." Knox said. "I'm saying, it's a consideration. You know, before you go full Terminator on this deal."

"Consider what, exactly?" Ronan asked. "That I should suddenly conjure a spouse and two-point-five children for the sake of appearances? Maybe throw in a minivan while I'm at it?"

"Whoa, whoa," Gabriel cut in. "Let's not get carried away here. Knox isn't saying you should start recruiting at school fundraisers."

"Not yet, anyway," Knox muttered under his breath, earning a sharp look from Ronan.

"Knox," Gabriel said, before turning his attention back to Ronan. "Look, all he's saying is that Beauchamp has a preference. It doesn't mean your deal's dead in the water. You're Ronan Wilder. If anyone can convince the guy that bachelorhood is the ultimate commitment to business, it's you."

"Exactly," Knox agreed. "You could probably sell him on the idea that being single makes you more focused. Heck, for all we know, he'll be begging you for tips by the end."

Ronan glanced between the two of them. He said no more, and the silence that followed felt heavy, filled with unspoken questions.

"Besides," Gabriel added, "it's not like you don't already have half the city convinced you're some kind of business messiah. Beauchamp's no different. Family man or not, he'll come around once he sees what you're bringing to the table."

"Messiah, huh?" Ronan said. "I'll remember that next time you ask me to cover your tab."

"Please do," Gabriel returned without missing a beat, lifting his glass in a toast. "To Ronan, savior of investments and reluctant backbone of Oath Capital."

"Reluctant is right," Ronan agreed, the hum of the restaurant around all around him. The clink of cutlery on plates, the low murmur of conversations, the laughter from a nearby table —it all blurred into background noise.

The phrase "family men" stuck in his mind like a splinter. This wasn't a minor inconvenience. It was a fracture in the system. Oath Capital didn't thrive on conventional expectations. It was powered by meticulous planning and reason, attributes that he took immense pride in delivering consistently.

"Earth to Ronan." Knox's voice broke through his spiraling thoughts. "You look like you're calculating how to overthrow a small government. Relax, man. We're here to eat overpriced entrees, not plot world domination."

"Speak for yourself," Ronan said, lowering his glass. "I'm always plotting."

"Yeah, I can tell." Knox gave him a knowing look. "The frown on your face is a trademark at this point. You should patent it before some other brooding billionaire steals your look."

Ronan was amused. "Noted."

"Seriously, though," Knox continued, "you're not gonna let some 'family man' nonsense get under your skin, are you? Beauchamp may want a picture-perfect investor, but we both know he cares more about returns. You've got this in the bag. And if not…" He paused, his look filled with humor. "I hear those rent-a-family services are popular these days."

"Knox." Gabriel chuckled, shaking his head. "Please stop giving him ideas. The last thing New York needs is Ronan orchestrating a fake family like it's a hostile takeover."

Knox threw up his hands. "I'm saying, options exist. Plus, I hear Golden Retrievers are excellent judges of character. Honestly, Ronan, it might be a win-win."

"Right," Ronan deadpanned. "Because nothing screams credibility like showing up to a meeting with a rented Labrador and a borrowed toddler."

"Don't knock it till you try it." Knox raised his glass with a wink. "Besides, you've already got the broody executive vibe down. Add a kid with big eyes and a tragic backstory, and Beauchamp will eat out of your hand."

"Let me guess," Ronan said wryly. "You got this brilliant plan from one of those Hallmark movies you pretend not to watch."

"Only for research," Knox claimed, unapologetic.

"Research," Gabriel echoed. "For what, exactly?"

"Life," Knox stated simply. "You never know when you might need to dump a bucket of charm on someone."

"Well, you certainly have enough to spare." Ronan's tone was laced with sarcasm. He leaned back in his chair, relaxed. For tonight, at least, he could let the question of Beauchamp—and his so-called preferences—rest in the back of his mind.

Chapter 4

ARM WEDGED with a travel mug that read "Coffee Is My Love Language," Devney faced the towering glass doors of Oath Capital. An oversized bag dragged down one shoulder, a precarious stack of files balanced in her free hand. The early morning wrapped around her, broken only by the faint hum of traffic and the rhythmic click of distant heels on pavement. Getting the door open was a clumsy juggle.

"Morning, Joe!" Her voice was bright as she approached the security guard, a grizzled veteran of the early morning shift, who gave her a nod.

"Your boss beat you in today."

Ronan Wilder, already in the office? She quickened her pace to the elevator, her thoughts tumbling over each other as fast as her pulse. The thought of him already settled at his desk sent a jolt of pure panic through her as she hurried toward her workspace outside his glass-walled office.

"Yes, Mr. Beauchamp…" His deep voice carried through the open door, clipped yet professional. "Of course, I comprehend the importance of traditional values…"

She paused mid-step. Traditional values? Did he even know what those were?

This was the same man who referred to holiday decorations as "seasonally mandated clutter."

She set her things on her desk, her gaze drifting back toward his office. He was pacing behind his desk, phone pressed to his ear. His tie—usually a perfect Windsor knot—hung askew, as if it had offended him. A hand raked through his dark hair, leaving it in a state of disheveled chaos she'd never witnessed.

"Yes." He stopped mid-stride. "I assure you, Mr. Beauchamp, Oath Capital is committed to upholding the highest standards. No, absolutely, I agree." His tone tightened, like someone trying to negotiate world peace while walking barefoot over Legos.

She bit her lip to suppress a grin as she sank into her chair. The usually unflappable CEO looked completely discombobulated. Usually he was a fortress of control, all crisp suits and focus. Today, he looked like a man facing an unexpected tax audit.

She turned to her monitor, booting up her computer. Habit, born from managing the whirlwind that was his schedule, had her pulling up the guest list for the upcoming charity gala. She wasn't officially on the distribution list, but she knew the right people. A well-timed request, a favor cashed in, and by last night, someone had forwarded her a copy.

As the spreadsheet loaded, her eyes skimmed the VIP section until they landed on a name she recognized: Beauchamp, Andrew. "Perfect." She leaned back in her chair, her voice low. This confirmed what she'd told Ronan— Beauchamp would indeed be there. Of course he'd be at this type of event. Old Money—capital O, capital M. The type of man who probably monogrammed his socks and folded his napkins into swans. No wonder Ronan was on edge. He was allergic to people whose hobbies included polo matches and judging other people's cufflinks.

Through the glass, she saw he had ceased pacing long enough to lean heavily against his desk. She couldn't discern the exact words anymore.

"Poor guy," she whispered. She didn't exactly feel sorry for him—he lived for high-stakes negotiations. Still, seeing him undone was rare enough to feel like she had spotted a unicorn in midtown. You knew it was probably a hallucination, but you had to stare, anyway.

The low murmur of his voice drifted through the glass walls of his office, then stopped abruptly. She took that as her cue. Grabbing the printed list from her desk, she crossed the short stretch to his door. A light knock on the frame preceded her entrance.

"Here's the final gala guest list." She held up the paper, hoping it might buy her a moment of goodwill.

He took it without hesitation, his sharp gaze scanning the names. "How did you get this?"

"I'm magical."

"Magical." He flipped through the pages. "That would explain the spell you've cast over my patience."

"Admit it. Your life would be dull without me."

"My life," he said quietly, still reading, "would be less chaotic without you."

"But so boring."

Only then did his focus turn to her. His eyes flicked up, the list momentarily forgotten, his expression darkening.

"Please tell me you're not planning to wear another sunflower creation to the gala."

She glanced down at her outfit—today's choice: a cheerful yellow blouse adorned with blooms, paired with cropped navy trousers. "What's wrong with sunflowers? They're happy flowers." Unbothered, she gave a little twirl for emphasis, the hem of her top fluttering.

"Happy flowers." He leaned back against his desk, appearing to brace himself for bad news, and loosened his already-askew tie further before sighing. "This isn't a garden party. It's a charity gala, a high-profile event. You need to dress like it's the Oscars, not an amateur botanical exhibit."

"Got it." She gave a solemn nod. "So, no meat dress like Gaga?"

He groaned. "Stop talking. I'm seriously reconsidering this whole arrangement."

"Don't worry." She waved a hand, unbothered. "I'll find clothes sparkly enough to make the old-money crowd swoon. Maybe an outfit with sequins and feathers." With a wink and a mock salute, she moved to leave, mission accomplished.

"Wait." His voice, hesitant and unfamiliar, stopped her mid-step.

She turned back slowly, one eyebrow raised. "Yes, Your Majesty?"

He ignored her teasing, standing straighter, arms crossed in a quiet barrier.

"I have a business proposition."

"Okay…" Her eyes narrowed with suspicion. "If this is about the coffee budget again, I swear—"

"It's not the coffee budget." He cut her off. "I need to know how you'd feel about becoming my fake fiancée."

Her brain seemed to freeze, refusing to process the words. She blinked. Once. Twice. Then a third time for good measure, because surely she had misheard. "Fake fiancée?"

"Fake fiancée." He stated.

"Did someone spike your morning espresso?" Nervous laughter bubbled up as she crossed her arms. "I think we should call HR."

"You're overreacting."

"Overreacting?" A sharp laugh escaped her. "You're asking me to be your fiancée. That's not an overreaction; that's basic insanity. This is like picking Comic Sans as your wedding font. Or drinking orange juice after brushing your teeth. It's crazy."

"Just—"

"Wait!" She raised a finger, her thoughts whirring. "Is this some kind of test? Should I be worried? Do you need therapy? Do I need therapy?"

"Close the door." His voice edged sharper, sounding like he was two seconds from ordering a hostile takeover.

"Why? Are you about to confess you've been secretly drinking before your nine a.m. meetings? Oh my God, is it kombucha? That would explain so much—" she rambled.

"Devney."

This time, his tone made her freeze, mid-gesticulation, her hand still hovering as if directing traffic. His expression was difficult to decipher, but behind his eyes—exasperation? Wariness? Maybe both. "Please. Close the door."

"Fine." She huffed, letting her arms fall dramatically to her sides as she turned back to his office door.

With a firm click, it closed. The air in the room suddenly felt thin, charged with the sheer craziness of what he'd just said.

"Thank you." His even tone returned, the slight looseness of his tie the only sign he might not be okay.

She crossed her arms, leaning a hip against the edge of his desk. "Explain."

"It's about Andrew Beauchamp."

"The billionaire with the estate on Martha's Vineyard? The one who looks like he stepped out of a Ralph Lauren catalog?"

"Yes. That Andrew Beauchamp. He's considering an investment in Oath Capital. A significant one. But he has… criteria."

"Criteria? Like what? Annual profits? Asset diversification?

Or does he make you recite Shakespeare while juggling flaming torches? Honestly, none of this would shock me at this point."

"Family values. He prioritizes working with businesses that represent traditional family values. Stability. Commitment. That sort of thing."

"And you think pretending to be engaged is going to check that box?"

"Exactly." His tone was as nonchalant as if they were discussing the stock market. "The Beauchamps will be at the charity gala this weekend—the same one you convinced me to attend specifically because Andrew would be there."

"The Beauchamps? As in, his wife will be there, too?"

"Indeed. Eleanor. She's known for her uncanny intuition. If I show up alone, it invites conjecture. But if I arrive with you by my side, it projects an image: stability, commitment, partnership."

"Or it suggests that you've lost your marbles." She threw her hands up. "This is insane. You can't just pencil in a fake engagement between 'Q3 Projections' and 'Order More Toner.'"

"Why not?" His calm confidence was infuriating. "It's strategic. Temporary. Mutually beneficial."

"Mutually beneficial?" Her voice rose. "What am I getting out of this? Besides the inevitable tabloid headlines and maybe an ulcer?"

He stepped closer. "You already manage every aspect of my life. Think of this as an extension of your current responsibilities."

"An extension? There's a difference between scheduling your dry cleaning and pretending to be your fiancée."

"Fake means temporary. Nothing more."

"Fine." She planted her palms on his desk, leaning in. "If I'm faking this engagement, we're negotiating terms."

He sat back, steepling his hands under his chin, and regarded her the way he probably looked at quarterly reports —calculating. "I'm listening."

"First off." She began ticking points off on her fingers. "I want a raise. A big one. Enough to cover the therapy I'll need after this circus."

"Done."

"Wait, really?"

"You're critically undervalued in your current role." He shrugged. "It's an overdue adjustment."

"Okay then." She spoke slowly. "Second, I want the corner office. You know, the one with the good view and the espresso machine nobody's allowed to use because it's 'for VIP guests only.'" She made air quotes with pointed sarcasm.

"Unnecessary for your position. But I'll approve weekly access to the espresso machine."

"Weekly?" she exclaimed. "What, do you think caffeine works on a subscription plan? Fine, moving on. Third, I'm going to need a new wardrobe."

"Why? You have clothes."

"Not fiancée-of-a-billionaire clothes." She gestured to her current attire. "Fake or not, I can't show up to these events looking like I stepped out of a Hallmark movie set in rural Wisconsin."

"Fair point." His mouth tightened as if admitting it pained him. "I'll authorize a reasonable shopping budget."

"Define 'reasonable.'" She crossed her arms.

"Reasonable." His tone was flat, offering no clarification.

"If I show up in an outfit bedazzled from the clearance rack, people are going to assume you're losing your touch. Do you want that kind of press?"

He sighed, muttering about being extorted in broad daylight, then said more clearly, "Fine. A generous shopping budget. No bedazzling required."

"Great." She straightened, brushing imaginary dust from her skirt. "Now let's talk about how this plan is destined to implode spectacularly."

"Implode?" He frowned, clearly unaccustomed to anyone predicting failure in his vicinity. "This has been strategically calculated."

"Sure, it has." She plopped into the chair across from him, gesturing. "Because nothing says 'calculated' like fake engagements."

She paused, eyes narrowing as the pieces connected. "Let me paint you a picture. Step one: Mr. Beauchamp does a background check. Guess what he finds? Your spotless life history suddenly comes with an extra—how convenient—fiancée who doesn't exist in any of your previous Christmas cards."

She leaned in, composed but focused. "You know, this whole thing isn't some meticulously thought-out plan. It's a reaction to what you said earlier, isn't it? You unraveled yourself with that 'family values' comment on the phone, and now this is the solution you came up with in a panic."

"Well, it's got to be easier than renting a family," he let slip.

She blinked, a laugh escaping her. "What?"

"Nothing. Let's move on."

"Okay, sure, whatever. Step two: social media. I don't know if you've noticed, but my Instagram is mostly dogs wearing sunglasses, and cupcakes I didn't bake. Suddenly, I've gone from 'quirky girl next door' to 'billionaire arm candy.' People will notice."

"Then delete it." He offered an infuriating shrug.

"Delete it?!" She stared at him as if he'd suggested she relocate to Mars. "Do you even hear yourself? That's digital sacrilege."

"These are minor obstacles." His voice dropped into that calm, collected CEO register that usually made interns quake in their loafers. "Eased by discretion and strategy."

"Strategy won't explain why you, Mr. Hermit Billionaire, are suddenly attending social functions with a girlfriend who appeared out of thin air," she shot back. "You hate people, remember? If this engagement is supposed to be believable, we're going to need to rewrite your entire personality."

"That seems excessive." His gaze narrowed for a moment.

"Excessive?" She laughed, a little too loudly. "The last time you willingly went to a party, it was probably catered by dinosaurs. No one will buy this unless you commit. And by 'commit,' I mean learn how to fake pleased expressions at strangers without looking like you're plotting their downfall."

"Anything else?" His expression was deadpan, as if she were rattling off a grocery list.

"Yeah." She stood, resting her hands on her hips. "We're going to need a backstory. A solid one. A romantic one." She fluttered her fingers in the air, as if sprinkling magic over the idea. "And no boring business metaphors. If I have to hear about synergy one more time, I'm throwing myself out the nearest window."

He remained silent.

She sighed. "Look, I've been in this office long enough for people to know I'm your assistant, not your…anything else. We need a story that convinces people we're more than work partners. Otherwise, this whole charade is going to unravel faster than a team-building exercise at happy hour."

"Noted. Are we finished here?" he asked, posture suggesting he hoped so.

"Not even close," she said, turning toward the door. But before she left, she tossed him one last glance over her shoulder. "Hope you're ready for some acting lessons, Romeo. This has the potential to be a spectacular disaster."

"Good thing I specialize in damage control." He picked up a pen, his voice composed as though this conversation hadn't flipped his meticulously ordered world upside down. "Let's—"

"Mr. Wilder?" Barbara from Legal appeared in the doorway, a stack of papers tucked under her arm

"Barbara." His tone shifted to the measured politeness usually reserved for legal counsel and tax auditors. "What can I do for you?"

"Contracts." Barbara stepped into the office as though she owned it, plunking the thick stack of documents onto his pristine glass desk. The sound reverberated like a tiny legal earthquake. "The merger paperwork needs your signature."

"Of course it does," he muttered. He glanced at Devney.

"Do you need me, or should I go back to my desk?".

"Yes," he began.

"Your presence isn't necessary," Barbara interjected.

"Great," Devney cut in quickly, slipping out before anyone could argue further. She closed the door behind her with the most professional amount of force possible—not quite a slam, but just enough to make a point.

She walked back to her desk, settling into her chair before glancing toward his office through the glass. He was already deep in discussion with Barbara, gesturing toward one of the contracts while the lawyer pointed out details with her pen. His tie remained loosened, his shirt sleeves rolled up to his elbows like some kind of overworked GQ model.

The man looked as if he hadn't slept in days, but somehow he still radiated that infuriating aura of competence.

"Fake fiancée." She shook her head. "Because that's totally normal workplace conversation."

But even as she thought it, her eyes drifted back to him. He was pacing now, likely explaining details in that clipped, businesslike tone that had a way of making even the most absurd ideas sound reasonable. She couldn't hear a word, but she could picture it perfectly.

And then the realization struck her—this might actually work.

She leaned back in her chair, crossing her arms as she considered the sheer lunacy of the situation. She already managed his calendar, his emails, his dry cleaning, and his coffee preferences depending on how grumpy he was that morning. How much harder could managing a fake engagement be? Sure, the potential for disaster was enormous, but wasn't that her specialty—wrangling chaos and making it appear well-orchestrated?

Through the glass, he looked up suddenly, catching her staring. For a split second, their eyes met. She ducked her head, pretending to be engrossed in whatever nonsense was on her screen—probably an email from HR about the potluck sign-up sheet. Very important stuff.

"Train wreck," she murmured, shaking her head. Still, a certainty shifted inside her—small but real. She looked back at the glass and whispered to herself, "if anyone can teach this man to fake romance, it's me."

$$\rule{6cm}{0.4pt}$$

Chapter 5

$$\rule{6cm}{0.4pt}$$

THE OFFICE WAS STILL in that eerie, after-hours way. The fluorescent lights buzzed overhead while phones and keyboards had fallen silent hours ago. He sat at the head of the conference table, laptop open, legal pad and Montblanc pen aligned. Across from him, she perched on the chair's edge, legs tucked beneath her with casual confidence.

"Thank you for staying late." His eyes remained on his screen.

"Of course." She spun her pen. "It's not every day your boss proposes a fake engagement." A grin touched her lips but vanished when he looked up at her. "I mean, happy to help."

"Good." He turned the laptop toward her, displaying meticulously formatted bullet points. "We need a consistent narrative—key milestones, dates, reasons for the relationship's progression. If we're going to convince Andrew Beauchamp, this story must hold under scrutiny."

"Milestones?" She tilted her head, golden hair catching the light. "Like when we first met? Or 'first time I forgot your coffee order.'"

"First meeting." He crossed his arms. "Noone forgets my coffee order."

"Right. Black, no sugar, no joy." She scrawled details at the top of the page in her loopy, colorful handwriting, her sparkly pen moving with exaggerated flair. "Okay, Mr. Logic, what's the plan?"

"Keep it simple. We met here. At work."

"Sure, but boring." She wrinkled her nose. "Can't we add some sparkle? A coffee-shop meet-cute?"

"That didn't happen," he stated flatly.

"But isn't the point to craft a story that's romantic and swoon-worthy?"

"Romance isn't the objective. Credibility is."

"Ronan." She gave him that imploring look that made him feel both challenged and oddly disarmed. "For people to believe this, it has to feel real. People aren't spreadsheets. Even Andrew Beauchamp."

"That's debatable," he returned, earning her laugh. He exhaled sharply. "Fine. But we still met at work. That's non-negotiable."

"Logical." She tapped her pen against her chin. "But not memorable. What if we started with a more serendipitous beginning? Like locking eyes across the room at a gala."

"I wouldn't have met you anywhere else but here." The words slipped out unchecked, landing like a pebble in still water, sending ripples through the space between them. She blinked, her pen pausing mid-tap. For once, she seemed at a loss for words, her bright, teasing demeanor dimmed by a more subdued quality.

"Well…" Her voice was quieter now when she finally spoke. "When you put it like that."

"Let's move on." His gaze dropped back to his laptop, though the air in the room felt different now, charged.

"Right. So…first date? Please tell me you're not going to say the office break room."

He looked at her. "Focus."

"Fine, fine." A laugh escaped her. "But if we're sticking to the truth, we need to add some color. No one will believe you swept me off my feet over spreadsheets."

"Why not?" He frowned. "It makes sense. It's logical."

"We're crafting a love story, not a business proposal. Love doesn't come with bullet points."

"I'd argue structure is what this needs." He maintained his position. "The truth is the strongest foundation."

"Sure." She tilted her head. "But even truth needs sparkle. What if we say you noticed me at one of those corporate parties you pretend to enjoy?"

"Pretend to enjoy?" He shot her a dry look.

"Picture it. You're brooding by the bar in your perfectly tailored suit, and then"—her voice took on a dramatic flair—"you see me under the chandelier, laughing, and everything changes."

"Everything changes," he repeated flatly.

"Too much?" She laughed. "But admit it—better than 'we met because you caught me stealing your stapler.'"

His gaze found hers, direct and sure. "Like I said before, I wouldn't have met you anywhere else but work." His voice dipped, low and even, and the truth of it hovered in the space between them.

She froze, her playful comment stopping before she said it. His words seemed to make the room go quiet.

"Well," she said after a beat, her expression shifting as she processed the underlying tone. She straightened, her spine stiffening, her voice cooler now, more distant. "I didn't realize we were that different."

He exhaled. "Not different, but from different circles."

Devney offered a small, tight smile. "Ah, circles. Right. Mine tend to be less…gilded, I suppose. More prone to glitter pens than golf courses."

"Let's move on. We still need to decide how long we claim we've been together."

A short, humorless laugh escaped her as she shook her head. "You know, if you can't even see this working, how is anyone else supposed to believe it?"

"We can be believable."

"Good. Then let's figure out how."

The conference room felt strangely cozy, a lamp casting light on the open notebook between them.

"Let me grab my sword and shield." Her pen was poised. "What's our first dragon to face?"

"Timing." His delivery was crisp. "He'll question why this is happening suddenly. He knows I don't make impulsive decisions."

"Which is why we lean into that. We tell him it's been building. We wanted to be sure before going public. You're measured, I'm practical—it fits."

He considered her answer. "Fine. But he'll also dig into how we met. You said earlier that he might not buy into an office romance."

"Good thing this isn't technically an office romance." A sly grin touched her lips. "It's a professional connection that blossomed outside work hours. Think of it as romantic overtime."

"Romantic overtime?" The corners of his lips curved.

"Yes. Trademark pending." She jotted a note. "Next objection?"

"Chemistry," he stated bluntly. "He'll want to see proof. Real moments that sell the relationship."

"Easy. We talk about inside jokes, quirks, how you actually smile when no one's looking."

"I don't smile," he corrected.

"Precisely. It's believable because it's realistic. And if he still doubts us, we dazzle him with a ridiculously romantic proposal story—one so swoony he won't question a thing."

"Right, the proposal," he said dryly. "Because that will be a breeze."

"We'll get there." Her confidence didn't waver. "Beauchamp won't know what happened. What else?"

He hesitated, drumming his fingers against the table. He wasn't sure if he was more irritated or impressed by how naturally she steered the conversation. Their rhythm was effortless —too effortless. He glanced at her, her expression lit by the lamplight, and felt an unsettling quality creep in. He recognized, with some discomfort, that he was starting to depend on her.

"Okay, time-out. My brain's officially fried." She dropped her pen and stretched dramatically. "We need food before we lose all sense of humanity."

Thirty minutes later, they were unpacking cartons of pad thai and spring rolls, the spicy-sweet aroma filling the room.

"All right." She spoke through a mouthful of noodles, unbothered by decorum. "Let's brainstorm proposal settings. Somewhere meaningful. Romantic. Memorable."

"Meaningful." He poked at a spring roll with his chopsticks. "We've known each other for six months. Define meaningful."

"Your lake house." Her suggestion came without hesitation as she set her takeout box aside. Her voice took on a quieter, wistful quality. "Think about it. Calm, close, only the two of us. Imagine the sun setting over the water, the whole place glowing gold. You'd have a ring in your pocket, nerves kicking in, and you'd go for it, no hesitation. No speeches, no grand gestures. Simple and real."

Her words made the scene so clear that for a moment he forgot it wasn't real. The lake house offered silence and solitude, its sunsets breathtaking. And the thought of standing there with her, caught in that golden light…

"Too much?" Her voice pulled him back.

"Not necessarily. It's isolated." He set his chopsticks down. "No through-roads, only a dirt path leading to the water. There's a dock, and sometimes people fish, but mostly it's peaceful. A good place to disappear if needed."

"Fishing?" Her voice rose an octave. "You? With a fishing pole? I need photographic evidence."

He pinched the bridge of his nose, his mouth twitching. "It was one time. In a rowboat, not waders."

"Even better!" She clasped her hands dramatically. "Please tell me you wore one of those vests with all the little pockets."

"You're impossible." His tone was dry, but he didn't deny it, which only encouraged her.

"So our fake engagement story involves the ever-dignified Ronan Wilder fumbling with fish and hooks?" A smile played on her lips.

"Not exactly." His voice was careful, city lights reflecting off his glasses. "I was twelve. My uncle insisted I learn 'life skills.' It became a disaster."

Her eyes lit up. "I have to hear this."

He sighed before relenting. " I caught a fish, panicked, and the line snapped. The fish flopped into the boat, and I nearly capsized us trying to escape it. My uncle had to save both me and the fish."

She burst out laughing. "I can see it—you, all gangly limbs, flailing while this poor fish—" She couldn't even finish.

"Are you done?" he asked, watching her.

"Not even close. This is gold. We have to use it." She spoke between giggles. "You take me fishing at the lake house, try to impress me, but history repeats. The fish goes rogue, and I heroically save the day."

"You heroically save the day?"

"Absolutely. I wrestle that fish into submission while you sit in awe. That's when you realize you can't live without me. Boom. Proposal." She grinned triumphantly.

"That's absurd."

"Absurdly charming." She pointed a takeout chopstick at him. "Which is why it's perfect. Trust me, people eat up this kind of thing. It makes you seem…human."

He went silent. Human. As if that was a trait he needed to work on. This ridiculous charade was already pushing his patience to its limit.

Apparently satisfied with his silence, she snapped her notebook shut with a flourish and pushed back her chair. "Well," she announced, rising to her feet, "I think that's enough fake romance for one night. Unless you've got any other thrilling details to add, like how we bonded over our mutual love of spreadsheets."

He watched her, debating whether to dignify that with a response.

For once, she said nothing, her gaze fixed on him, thoughtful. The oversized conference room felt different, like the air had shifted around them.

"I think we've exhausted all angles." He leaned back. "You did a good job."

She froze mid-motion, her bag half-slung over her shoulder, then turned to him, her expression filled with feigned disbelief. "Was that—" She gasped dramatically, clutching a hand to her chest. "A compliment? From you? Stop the presses."

"Don't get used to it."

"Noted." She grinned at him, wide and easy. "Goodnight, boss man. Try not to overthink this whole 'pretend to love me' thing. You'll sprain a muscle."

"Goodnight," he said.

She lingered a second longer than necessary, her eyes sweeping over him as if weighing unspoken words before deciding against them. Then, with a playful wink, she turned and walked away. The door swung shut behind her.

He sat still, staring at the vacant space where she'd been only moments ago.

The room felt bigger now. Colder.

"Just business."

Chapter 6

SHE YANKED another dress off the rack, its sequins catching the harsh fluorescent lighting of the boutique. "This one's shiny?" she said weakly, holding it up for Lucy's inspection.

Lucy recoiled like the dress had insulted her. "Unless you're planning to blind everyone at the gala, no. Hard pass."

Devney shoved it back onto the overcrowded rack with a groan.

"Why are we doing this today?" Lucy asked. "The gala is literally tonight."

"I've been busy. With work. With fake-fiancée-ing. With managing the slow unraveling of my mental stability. Take your pick."

Lucy plopped onto a nearby velvet pouf, crossing her legs and propping her chin on her hand like she was watching a live rom-com train wreck. "This is your karma for agreeing to get fake-engaged to your boss. Seriously, Dev, what were you thinking? 'Oh sure, Ronan Wilder, my emotionally constipated billionaire boss, needs a fiancée—sounds fun!'"

"First," she said, rifling through another rack without

looking at her friend, "he's not emotionally constipated. He's selectively expressive."

"Selective is right," Lucy said with a snort. "He expresses himself to spreadsheets and quarterly reports, not humans."

"Second," she said, ignoring the jab, "this is a strategic partnership, okay? I help him close this deal with the Beauchamps, and he doesn't fire me for accidentally CC'ing his mother on the email about her cat. Everybody wins."

"Strategic partnership. You realize how bananas that sounds, right?"

"Yes, but it's well-dressed bananas. Or at least it will be if we find me a dress," she said, pulling a slinky black gown from the rack. Before Lucy could protest, she disappeared into the fitting room.

A minute later, she emerged, the black gown turning her reflection in the mirror into an image out of a red-carpet event. The fabric hugged her figure, the neckline plunging enough to be daring without straying into scandalous territory.

"Wow," Lucy said, sitting up straighter. "Okay, I take it back. That's not bananas. That's an entire gourmet banana sundae, top shelf."

"Right?" She twirled, the hem swishing. "Who knew I had this in me?"

"Everyone except you," Lucy said, deadpan. Then her eyes narrowed, and she pointed at Devney's bare left hand. "Wait. What are you doing for a ring? Please don't tell me Ronan sprung for a monstrosity shaped like a stock portfolio."

"Funny you should mention that," she said, digging into her purse. After a few seconds of rummaging, she pulled out a garish sunflower-shaped ring.

"Ta-da!" she said, sliding it onto her finger with a showy little wave. "Problem solved."

Yellow stones surrounded a cluster of white ones in the

center, with brown gems forming the petals. It was loud. It was clunky. It was hideous. It was her.

Lucy stared, then doubled over laughing so hard she nearly rolled off the pouf. "You cannot be serious. That thing looks like you mugged a kindergartener at craft time."

"Hey, desperate times call for desperate accessories," she said, admiring the ring. "Besides, it's got character. And until Mr. Billionaire decides otherwise, this is as good as it gets."

"Good luck explaining that to the Beauchamps," Lucy said.

Two hours later, Devney ran a hand over the front of her gown in her tiny apartment's entryway. She glanced at the clock, wondering if Ronan had gotten lost between his penthouse and her decidedly less glamorous building. As she debated texting him, a sharp knock echoed at the door.

"It's time," she said softly, taking a deep breath and opening the door.

He exuded his usual unruffled elegance, the crisp lines of his flawlessly tailored black tuxedo emphasizing his composed presence. Yet for a man who prided himself on restraint, his composure wavered as his eyes swept over her. His focus lingered on her face before drifting downward, tracing the graceful silhouette of her gown. His expression gentled for an instant—unguarded, rising and fading in a breath.

"Well?" she asked, fidgeting as the silence dragged on.

"Acceptable," he said at last, though the faint roughness in his voice betrayed him.

"Wow, calm down with the compliments," she said, stepping aside to let him in. His attention dipped to her left hand.

"Is that..." His eyes narrowed, gears visibly turning as he pointed at the sunflower ring like it might sprout legs and run. "Is that all you have?"

"You don't pay me enough to purchase priceless baubles," she said breezily, holding up her hand to admire the ring like it belonged in a museum. "This is the best I've got—fifteen ninety-nine at the corner drugstore."

"Incredible," he said. Yet as his eyes returned to her, his expression softened—a shift, barely perceptible, but there.

"It'll have to do," he said finally, his voice low and resigned. He straightened his jacket, then wordlessly held out her coat. She slid into it, and for a second, he didn't let go, his hands resting heavily on her shoulders as they both stared at their reflections in the mirror. It was a silent acknowledgement of the charade they were about to walk into. He glanced at the door and said, "Let's go."

The ballroom was a dazzling spectacle, awash with twinkling chandeliers, gleaming champagne flutes, and guests who seemed to have been born in designer couture. She adjusted her hair for the fifth time, fingers lingering as she tried to find an expression that felt believable.

The sunflower ring flashed defiantly under the lights, a bold statement of rebellion sparkling on her finger.

"Relax," he said quietly beside her, his tone even but low enough that only she could hear it. "You're fidgeting."

"Some of us don't spend our evenings parading through events like this," she said, tilting her head just enough to maintain a pleasant expression for the passing couples who glanced their way.

"Keep your expression pleasant," he said, his lips barely moving. He'd been doing that all night—talking without breaking his polished exterior. It was maddeningly effective. "And remember, you're madly in love with me."

"Madly," she said, taking a sip of her champagne. The bubbles fizzed against her tongue, which was nice because it distracted her from how close his arm was to hers. He kept her near his side all evening, his hand resting on the small of her back whenever anyone approached. It was so effortless she could believe he didn't hate every second of this.

"Here they come," he said suddenly, his voice tightening. His attention flicked toward an elegant couple weaving through the crowd. Even before they reached them, she knew who they were.

Eleanor Beauchamp moved with effortless poise, her sharp eyes fixed on them, intense, missing no detail. Beside her, Andrew Beauchamp strolled with casual authority, his expression kind yet measured, as if his full appraisal of them was complete before he even spoke.

"Showtime," she said under her breath, her fingers curling instinctively around the delicate stem of her champagne flute.

"Devney." His voice was firm, pulling her focus before the Beauchamps arrived. For once, there was no sharpness—only a calm, unwavering certainty. Almost reassuring. "You've got this."

And with barely a moment's pause, as Eleanor and Andrew stopped before them, she embraced the role with a sudden, natural confidence. "Mr. and Mrs. Beauchamp! What an absolute pleasure."

"You must be Devney." Eleanor's voice was a perfect mix of intrigue and decorum. She extended her hand to Ronan with genuine interest. "And you must be Mr. Wilder. Eleanor Beauchamp. Andrew has been looking forward to this conversation." She glanced between them with curiosity. "And what a lovely companion you've brought."

Devney hadn't said a word when Ronan stepped in. His tone was decisive but not harsh as he said, "She is more than my companion." He reached out to take her hand. "She's my fiancée."

"Congratulations," Andrew said before shaking his hand. Then he turned his attention to her. His expression was pleasant, but the calculation behind it was hard to miss. "So, how did you two meet?"

She was prepared for this. "Ah, the classic question," she

said, buying a moment with another sip of champagne. She glanced up at Ronan, who gave her one of those maddeningly neutral expressions—just enough movement to say, *Go on, let's see how you spin this.* Somehow, what they had planned didn't seem to fit the bill, so she improvised.

"Actually," she said, laughter slipping out as she spoke, "it's more of a sitcom than a fairy tale. We first met when I started working for him. Strictly professional, of course. But after spending long hours together, putting out corporate fires, and navigating his unique approach to teamwork, the dynamic sort of evolved. Against all odds."

She glanced at him, eyes twinkling. "Somewhere between crisis management and coffee runs, we realized we were more than a capable duo. And, well…" She shrugged, as if the rest were obvious. "On our first official date, I drenched his immaculate white shirt with a full glass of merlot." She tipped her head toward him with a cheeky grin.

Eleanor's eyebrows shot up. "Really?"

Her grin turned shameless, mischief bright in her eyes. "Oh, absolutely. And then there was the time I accidentally locked us out of his lake house in the middle of winter. We had to spend the night in the boathouse until the locksmith could make it out the next day."

A burst of laughter escaped Andrew as he looked at Ronan. "Sounds like you two have had quite the journey."

Laughter bubbled around her as she said, with a playful wink at her "fiancé," "And yet, despite all these mishaps, he still proposed to me. Can you imagine? He actually wants someone who brings this level of spontaneity into his life." Her laugh rang light and easy, but when she glanced at him, her expression softened.

Andrew chuckled. "Well now, it certainly appears she keeps you on your toes, Ronan. That can't be all bad."

"She's worth it," he said, his voice even, so composed and

certain that her heart gave a small, startled jump. Then, as if it were the most natural thing in the world, he slid an arm around her waist and drew her closer. His palm pressed against the thin fabric of her dress, sending a quick shiver through her.

Eleanor's sharp eyes flicked between them, dissecting every nuance, every exchanged look, every movement. For a moment, the ballroom's buzz dimmed…the world shrank to just the four of them. She swallowed, mind racing for her next move.

Then, without thinking it through, she leaned into him, letting her head rest against his shoulder.

He stiffened for half a second—long enough for her to notice—but then relaxed, his hand shifting at her waist. When he spoke, his voice was quieter, lower, carrying an intimacy that made her breath catch.

"She makes life interesting," he said, barely above a murmur.

Eleanor's lips curved, though her eyes still gleamed with interest. "Interesting is often underrated," she said, before glancing at Andrew. "Don't you agree, darling?"

"Certainly keeps things lively," Andrew said, raising his glass in a silent toast.

Devney straightened, maintaining her calm facade as though nothing about that exchange had set her heart pounding. As the conversation flowed, she stole a glance at Ronan. His composed demeanor held, yet a new tension edged his posture, as if he too had registered the shift.

Eleanor's gaze dropped to Devney's hand, and her stomach plummeted. The ring. She'd been so focused on charm and wit that she'd forgotten about the sunflower perched on her finger like an uninvited party crasher.

It sat there, bold and unapologetic, its cheerful yellow petals clashing spectacularly with the elegance of the evening. A statement piece, certainly—not the kind that said wealth and sophistication. More like whimsical flea-market find.

"That's an interesting choice," Eleanor said, polite interest threading her tone as her eyes lingered on the yellow-and-brown sparkle.

Devney didn't miss a beat. "Oh, he picked it out himself," she said, lifting her hand, so the light caught the gaudy stones. "Very sentimental."

"Sentimental?" Eleanor repeated. "Unexpected."

"Absolutely," she said, easing into a sliver of truth. "He knew I wouldn't appreciate the typical choice."

She sent him a playful glance from beneath her lashes, fingers tracing the sunflower circle.

More than an emblem of their faux engagement, the ring stirred sun-drenched memories of her grandmother's homestead—golden fields, laughter on the breeze—little pieces of home she hadn't realized she missed until she spotted the ring at the corner store. Fifteen ninety-nine felt like a small price for a thread back to that warmth.

With a curve to her lips, she turned to Eleanor. "Sunflowers remind me of someone special—my grandmother, who raised me after my mother passed away," she said, her tone tender as she held the other woman's gaze. "I wear them because they make me feel closer to her, even though she's been gone for years."

Then, as if the moment hadn't dipped into inconvenient honesty, she nudged him with her elbow. "Isn't that right?"

He adjusted a cufflink as though the turn in conversation were a routine pivot. "She has a unique way of tying the past to the present," he said. His lips curved, not quite a smirk, but close, meant only for her.

"Family values. That's what I like to see," Andrew said, gently swirling his bourbon. His blue eyes glimmered with approval as he looked between them. "Not many men understand the importance of uniqueness in a partnership."

"He's not most men," Devney said, patting Ronan with theatrical affection and feeling the brief tension in his muscles.

"Clearly," Eleanor said, her expression unreadable. Then she laughed, a genuine sound that caught Devney off guard. "Well! They're not what I expected. I like it."

"Me, too," Andrew said, tipping his glass before taking a sip.

Devney exhaled as the tension in her shoulders eased. Eleanor had relaxed, and Andrew's scrutiny had melted into amused approval. It felt like stepping off a roller coaster and realizing she was still in one piece.

"Shall we discuss that proposal over lunch next week?" Andrew asked Ronan, casual but decisive.

"Of course," Ronan said, sliding smoothly back into businessman mode. He extended a hand, which Andrew shook. "Devney will call Monday to confirm the details."

"Wonderful," Eleanor said brightly, her eyes lingering on Devney a heartbeat longer before she turned with her husband.

The second they were out of earshot, Devney let out the tiniest, most dignified sigh. "Unique, huh?" she said, glancing up at him with a sly grin.

"Unbelievable," he said under his breath, with no real bite. If anything, he looked a little impressed.

Or maybe she imagined it. Either way, she wasn't about to let him ruin her moment.

"Admit it," she said, linking her arm through his as they made their way toward the bar. "You'd be lost without me."

"Don't push your luck."

Later, as the night wound down, and the crowd thinned, he handed her a glass of champagne.

"You deviated from the script, but you pulled it off."

"*We* pulled it off," she said, clinking his glass.

"I'll admit it." He lifted his own. "You're good at this."

"Good? Try exceptional."

"Don't get cocky."

"Wouldn't dream of it." She glanced sideways at him, catching the slight lift of his mouth and the glint of unspoken thoughts in his eyes, and she knew she'd won more than Eleanor and Andrew's approval tonight.

Chapter 7

THE SILENCE in the car was heavy with the residue of their performance. Streetlights painted fleeting stripes across Ronan's knuckles as he gripped the steering wheel, his movements tense. The air still hummed with the ghosts of shared laughter and feigned intimacy from the gala, leaving a charged void that neither of them seemed willing to fill. He could still feel the phantom weight of her hand on his arm, the scent of her perfume—citrus and pear, a bright splash in his sterile world—clinging to the fabric of his suit.

It had been a role, a performance.

So why did his pulse quicken every time he caught her scent lingering on his jacket? Why did the words "my fiancée" roll off his tongue when he spoke to Andrew Beauchamp, natural as breathing? The memory surfaced unbidden. Devney was spinning her story about the sunflower ring, her eyes bright with invented history, her voice carrying such conviction that he'd found himself leaning forward, drawn into her fiction. In that moment, she hadn't been his assistant fielding a crisis. She'd been a woman weaving magic from thin air, and he'd wanted to step inside her story and make it real.

"Well," Devney said, her voice quiet in the confined space. "I think they bought it. You're a surprisingly good actor, Mr. Wilder."

A muscle jumped in his jaw. The compliment landed like a critique. He was a good actor because his entire life was an act—a carefully curated performance of control. But tonight had been different. Tonight had felt dangerously like truth.

"The role wasn't demanding," he said, his gaze fixed on the road ahead.

"Wasn't it?" She turned in her seat, the movement slight but her focus on him absolute. "You had to pretend to be in love with me. For a man who refers to joy as an 'inefficient allocation of emotional resources,' I'd say that was a stretch."

He didn't respond. He couldn't. The most difficult part of the night wasn't pretending to be in love with her—it was remembering, with increasing difficulty, that he was supposed to be pretending. Seeing the Beauchamps together—their easy rhythm, the unspoken understanding in a shared glance—had been like staring through a window into a world he'd deemed illogical and therefore unattainable.

"They have a genuine partnership," she said softly, as if hearing the echo of his thoughts. "The way they look at each other, it's like they're on the same team."

"No marriage is perfect," he said, the words automatic, a shield he'd carried since he was a boy.

"Maybe not perfect," she conceded, her voice gentle. "But it can be good. They respect each other."

"My parents' divorce left more scars than memories." The words left him before he could stop them, dragged from a place he kept locked and barricaded.

The statement hung between them, stark and heavy.

"How old were you?" she finally asked, her voice calm in the dim car.

"Twelve." Old enough to understand, young enough to be rewired by it.

A delivery truck swerved in front of them, and he braked hard.

"It was acrimonious," he added, the word inadequate.

He could still hear the precise, cutting tone of his mother's voice on the phone with her lawyer, discussing him as if he were an asset being divided. "The visitation schedule is non-negotiable," she'd said, her voice like ice, while he sat at the top of the stairs, pretending not to listen.

"They were two intelligent people using their knowledge of each other as weapons. I wasn't a witness to their war—I was ammunition. My father tallied the financial cost of every visit. My mother documented every minute he was late."

He risked a glance at her. The passing streetlights illuminated a profound empathy in her eyes. It made him want to say more, to unburden himself in a way he never had.

"They turned love into a zero-sum game," he finished. "Whoever cared less held all the power."

"And you learned from them," she said. It wasn't an accusation.

It was recognition, understanding. And it was more devastating than any judgment could have been.

"I learned that emotional investment is a liability," he confirmed, his throat tight. "In business, that clarity has served me well."

"And outside of business?" she asked, the question so simple, so direct, it disarmed him completely.

He thought of his sterile apartment, his hollow social interactions, his life devoid of the messy, unpredictable reality of genuine connection.

"Outside of business," he said, "it's been efficient."

She was silent for a long moment, the city lights sliding

over her face as she processed his admission. "That explains so much," she said, her voice barely a whisper.

His hands tightened on the wheel. "Explains what?"

"Why you keep everyone at such a careful distance," she said. "You build walls so high you can't see over them. You push away anyone who might try to climb them. Even people who care about you."

The car rolled to a stop outside her brownstone. The engine hummed, her words hanging in the air between them.

He turned to look at her, really look at her, for the first time since they'd left the gala. The sunflower ring on her finger caught the glow from a streetlamp. A fake ring for a fake promise that had just unearthed the most real part of him.

"Is that what you do?" he asked, his voice rough with an emotion he couldn't name. "Care about me?"

She held his gaze, her green eyes steady and deep, searching his face as if she could read the truth written there.

"Yes," she said. "I do."

A current, both alarming and exhilarating, shot through him. Without a word, he shut off the engine. He exited, circled to her side and opened her door, the movement stiff, unpracticed.

She looked up, startled, before accepting the gesture and stepping onto the curb. They walked up the short flight of stairs to her front door in silence, the city's hum a distant roar. She fumbled for her keys, her fingers clumsy. When the lock clicked, she turned, her back pressed against the door, trapped between him and the entrance.

"Ronan." she started, but his name trailed off as he took a step closer.

He was too close. He knew he was too close. He could see the faint pulse at the base of her throat, smell the lingering scent of her perfume. His hand lifted, driven by a need so sharp it stole his breath. His fingers hovered inches from her cheek, the space between them crackling with unspoken words and untapped want. He could feel the warmth radiating from her skin. Touch her. The command was primal. Don't. This crosses a line. What line? There are no lines anymore.

He dropped his hand, the small movement feeling like a defeat.

"Goodnight, Devney," he said, the words tight.

He turned and walked away without looking back, the image of her standing in the doorway—stunned, beautiful, and achingly real—burned into his mind. He didn't leave right away. He waited in his car at the curb, watching until the light in her window flickered on, a small beacon in the darkness.

Driving back to his empty penthouse, he realized with startling clarity that the carefully constructed architecture of his life had been compromised. She had found a crack in the foundation. And for the first time, he was terrified he didn't have a blueprint to fix it.

Chapter 8

THE BELL above Lucy's bakery door chimed its usual sing-song greeting as Devney stepped inside, the scent of cinnamon and fresh bread wrapping around her like a comforting hug. It was early, and the shop was still waking up, much like she was. Her mind was foggy, stuck somewhere between the gala and the reality of this morning.

Behind the counter, Lucy was already in full baker mode, dusted in flour, sleeves pushed up, hands moving with a steady rhythm as she worked a ball of dough. Her dark hair was piled atop her head in a messy bun, wisps escaping to soften the sharp edges of her expression. She looked up, and a wide grin bloomed across her face.

"Well, look what the cat dragged in." She flicked a glance at her friend over the ball of dough. "You're glowing. Which either means you won the lottery this morning, or—" She paused, flour-covered fingers stopping mid-knead, "—you're in love with your fake fiancé."

Devney's heart stuttered at the accusation, heat rising to her cheeks. She scoffed—maybe with a little too much force—

as she dropped onto her usual stool at the counter. The wooden seat creaked beneath her, familiar and grounding.

"First, rude. Second, this is the glow of a woman who got seven hours of sleep and had an ordinary morning." The lie felt awkward and unconvincing in her mouth. She'd deliberately not called Lucy on Sunday, and ignored her two calls, knowing a play-by-play of the gala would only cement how not-ordinary things had become. In reality, she'd spent the last two nights replaying every glance, every touch, every moment of tenderness in his voice at the gala.

Lucy didn't even look up, her hands moving through the dough. "Right. And I'm the type of person who minds my own business." She pressed her thumb into the dough like it had personally offended her.

Lucy folded the dough one last time before covering it with a cloth. She wiped her hands thoroughly on a towel, then reached into the display case for a scone. She slid it across to Devney on a small plate. "So, how was the party?"

Devney leaned her elbows on the counter, drawn to the heat still clinging to the pastry as its buttery aroma mingled with the cinnamon-sugar topping. She pretended to be interested in the scone. Anything to avoid her friend's too-perceptive gaze.

"It was fine. You know, champagne, small talk, obscenely expensive dresses." She shrugged, aiming for nonchalance and landing somewhere closer to suspicious evasion.

Lucy braced her hands on the counter, her stare so intense it made Devney want to squirm. "Try again. Because you bit your lip the way you do when you're pretending a big deal wasn't a big deal—when it absolutely was."

Devney let out a deep sigh. "It was. Fun." She winced at her own admission, as if the word itself was dangerous. "Okay, not fun, but better than I expected. He was different. More relaxed. He—he actually made jokes, Lucy. Jokes!"

The memory of his low laugh beside her ear made a shiver run through her. It had been a private sound, meant only for her, something she'd felt through the thin fabric of her dress where his hand had rested on the small of her back.

Lucy snorted. "The same Ronan who once told you that 'office humor undermines productivity?' That Ronan?"

"I know!" She threw her hands up, nearly knocking over her untouched coffee. "But he was different. We were talking to the Beauchamps, and everything was going well, and then—I don't know. It felt easy. Like we weren't faking it."

His arm around her waist seemed to belong there. Like the way he'd said "She's worth it" wasn't only for show. Like the silent drive home afterward, the way he'd actually opened up to her about his parents, meant more than their elaborate charade.

"That's because you weren't faking it."

"Don't start," Devney said, pointing at her with a butter knife, a weak attempt to ward off a truth she didn't want to admit. "It was good acting."

"Mmm-hmm." Lucy leaned forward, her eyes bright with interest and a hint of worry. "Tell me, did he dance with you? Did he stand a little too close? Did his eyes linger a little too long when he thought no one was watching?"

Her stomach flipped at how accurately Lucy had guessed. Different moments flooded her memory—his fingertips pressed against her dress, his breath brushing against her neck, feather-light and close, the moment when his eyes had met hers after she'd told the Beauchamps about her grandmother's sunflowers. Something had shifted between them in that instant, something that made her heart race even now, sitting safely in Lucy's bakery with the morning light streaming through the windows.

"You're imagining things," she said quietly, breaking off a

piece of scone without eating it. "And enjoying it way too much."

"Am I?" Lucy said, her voice quieter now, more concerned than teasing. "Because, Dev, you're sitting here in my bakery, looking like a woman who got twirled around a ballroom by a billionaire and actually enjoyed it."

She fumbled for words, opening her mouth, then snapping it shut when nothing coherent came out. Lucy had a way of digging into things she wasn't ready to examine, of forcing her to look at feelings she had tried to keep hidden, even from herself. The truth was, she had enjoyed last night—more than she should have, more than was safe.

She'd liked the feel of his hand on her back, the surprising softness in his eyes when he'd looked at her, the way his voice had softened when it was only the two of them. She'd liked feeling like they were a team, navigating the crowded ballroom together. She'd liked it, and that terrified her.

"Oh, look, croissants! Let's focus on those."

Lucy rolled her eyes but let it go—for now. "Fine. Be in denial. But just so you know, the longer you pretend this is all business, the harder it'll be when reality catches up."

The words landed with a heavy weight. She tried to brush them aside, but they settled deep, impossible to ignore. What if she was in denial? What if this charade was becoming more than business, at least for her? What would happen when it inevitably ended?

The bakery door swung open, and a rush of morning customers spared her from answering. She grabbed her coffee, muttered a quick goodbye, and slipped out before Lucy could dismantle her defenses any further.

Outside, the morning air was crisp with the bite of autumn. She walked briskly, her thoughts jumbled with each hurried step. Lucy's words echoed in her mind, a warning she couldn't quite silence. *The longer you pretend, the harder it gets.*

Was she pretending? Or was there real emotion growing beneath the surface of their arrangement? She thought of his rare moment of vulnerability in the car after the gala, the way he'd opened up about his parents, about never having seen a good marriage. It had felt genuine, like a glimpse of the real person he kept guarded. Like he was letting her see parts he kept hidden from everyone else.

As she approached the gleaming glass entrance of Oath Capital, she paused, catching her reflection in the polished surface—her cheeks flushed from the walk.

Get it together, Sinclair. This is business, not a romance novel.

With a deep breath, she steeled herself and pushed through the door, the hum of the office surrounding her. Normalcy, she thought. This is my normal life. The gala was an anomaly, a performance, nothing more.

But as she moved through the office, the world felt different —as if everything was slightly off-kilter.

He stood outside his office, arms crossed, waiting for her. He looked like himself again, all business, no trace of the vulnerability he'd shown when he drove her home that night, sharing pieces of his past in the quiet of his car.

"We have a problem," he said, his voice clipped.

"Good morning to you too." She set her things on her desk. "What kind of problem?"

"Eleanor Beauchamp invited us to spend the weekend at their estate. The entire weekend. On Martha's Vineyard."

"She did *what*?"

"Apparently, she was so charmed by us at the gala that she's eager to spend more time together." He rubbed a hand over his jaw. "Which means we have to continue this charade for an entire weekend, under the watchful eyes of the Beauchamps."

A weekend. With him. Pretending to be engaged. Panic and anticipation rose inside her. An entire weekend of more moments like when the line between real and pretend blurred beyond recognition.

She let out a low whistle. "Wow. The upper crust is buying it."

"This is serious, Devney. If we screw this up, Beauchamp could pull his interest."

"Relax, Wilder. I've got this. We'll be the perfect fake couple. But you need to work on your affectionate husband-to-be act."

"I don't do affectionate," he said flatly.

Liar, she thought, remembering the feel of his hand on her back, the way he'd looked at her when she talked about her grandmother.

"Then you'd better learn fast." She patted his arm before walking around her desk, ignoring the spark that jumped from his arm to her fingertips. "If we're leaving Friday, you have time to find clothes less intimidating. Maybe a sweater."

"I don't wear sweaters."

"That's my point," she said, but he had already walked away. And there. As she settled into her chair, she realized Lucy's words from that morning kept replaying in her mind. *The longer you pretend.*

She reached for her keyboard. This was business. Plain and simple.

She had to believe that. Because if she didn't, if she let herself think, even for a second, that some part of this was real, she would never get through it without getting hurt in the end.

And it would end once he secured Beauchamp's investment. Then back to boss and assistant. The thought created an unexpected ache inside her.

Through the glass walls of his office, she could see him at his desk, his attention fixed on his computer screen. He looked the same—focused, in control, a man whose world ran on precision and calculation. But she knew better now. She'd seen beneath the surface, the past hurts that formed him, the things that motivated him.

And that knowledge was dangerous. Because it made him a man with scars, fears, and moments of tenderness.

A man she might fall for.

The thought sent a jolt of fear through her. Falling for him wasn't part of the plan.

But as she forced herself to answer emails, schedule meetings, and check off the tasks that made up her day—another thought surfaced. Plans change. Hearts change. People change.

Footsteps approached, then stopped at the edge of her desk. He cleared his throat. "We'll review strategy tonight."

"Right," she said, matching his brisk tone. "Strategy. Actual couples don't need to review strategies for spending time with friends, you know."

"We're not a real couple," he said.

"Obviously. I'm making a point."

"Make it less ambiguously next time," he said, turning to head back to his office. But he paused at the doorway.

"And thank you. You were effective."

Effective. Like a new software update. Not charming, not the woman who'd made him laugh for what felt like the first time in years. Effective.

"Anytime," she said, her voice lighter than she felt. "That's what you pay me for,"

He disappeared into his office, leaving her alone with her thoughts.

Chapter 9

THEY AGREED to iron out the details at 5:30, so when Devney met him downstairs, he said, "Let's go."

She hesitated for half a second, then followed without question.

He'd chosen the restaurant strategically. Not only was it where he would meet Knox and Gabriel later, but it served multiple purposes—exclusive enough for privacy yet prestigious enough to be seen by the right people. Combining these meetings saved time and eliminated additional travel. The efficiency pleased him.

As they walked through the heavy oak doors, he watched her reaction from the corner of his eye. Her steps faltered as she took in the surroundings: dark wood paneling that absorbed the light, private leather booths that promised seclusion, crystal decanters sparkling behind the bar. A place designed for men with power and the discretion to use it wisely.

Her gaze moved over the space, he could almost see her taking mental notes, cataloging the kind of place this was—a setting where strategies were drawn in Scotch and fortunes sealed with handshakes. Her eyes narrowed at the far corner, where a senator sat deep in conversation with a tech CEO whose face regularly appeared on magazine covers.

She slid into the booth across from him, still scanning the room like someone collecting intel.

"Do you eat here often?" she asked, fingers drumming a rhythm against the polished tabletop.

"Often enough." He signaled to the server without looking. The man appeared in a moment. Everything here operated with meticulousness, without unnecessary conversation or delay.

She picked up the menu and set it down. "This place screams, 'I have more money than you, and I'd like you to know it.'"

He didn't bother looking up from his phone, where he was silencing an incoming call from Tokyo. "It's discreet."

"And outrageously overpriced."

"That too." He set his phone face down and gave her his full attention. They had bigger things to discuss than her outrage over a twenty-eight-dollar salad.

"The Beauchamps bought the story, but we can't afford any gaps. If they're inviting us deeper into their circle, it means more eyes. More questions."

She nodded. "So we keep it clean. Lake-house proposal, the wine spill, the corporate fire that sparked our star-crossed love. All still in play."

His jaw tightened at that last part. The thought of staging more romantic moments—touches, looks, the kind of heat that passed for real affection—hit uncomfortably close to home. It wouldn't be entirely an act. Now he was acutely aware of her laugh, her scent, the green in her eyes.

"We keep it simple," she said "They want a believable story. We've already given them one."

He nodded once. "You were sharp at the gala."

"I'm always sharp."

They spent a few more minutes reviewing the edges—her ring, his supposed moment of realization, and how they'd answer if someone asked about holidays, fights, or favorite takeout. The exchange was efficient. She asked smart questions. He gave succinct answers. They functioned as a well-oiled machine.

Midway through, his eyes caught on the small pendant on her neck. A delicate sunflower charm, winking in the low light. He'd seen it before. It used to irritate him—too sentimental. Now he knew why she wore it. It was part of her—a reminder of a grandmother who'd raised her to be stubborn, principled, and strong.

"So, clothing," she said. "I need to go shopping before we leave. I'm assuming I can't wear my usual wardrobe to a weekend with the Beauchamps."

"No." The answer was immediate. He pictured her in her typical work attire—bright sunflower prints, loud patterns, bedazzled accessories. "You'll need formal wear for dinner, casual for the vineyard tour, and daywear for brunch and sailing."

"Sailing?" Her voice pitched up.

"Yes. From what I've heard, these weekends are rigorous. Sailing is only the beginning. I've studied Andrew Beauchamp's business patterns and his social dynamics."

"Fine." She shook her head, then pointed at him. "But you're coming shopping with me."

"Why?"

"Because if I'm playing the role of your devoted fiancée, I need to wear clothing you'd approve of. Unless you want me showing up in a sundress with little sailboats on it."

The image almost made him laugh. Almost.

"I have no idea what people like the Beauchamps consider appropriate attire," she added. "Country-club casual? Yacht formal? Old money pretending to be modest but in thousand-dollar jeans? You'll have to translate."

"Fine. I'll go." She had a point. Every detail mattered.

"Great." Her eyes brightened. "Tomorrow after work? I know a boutique downtown."

"I have a better idea." He was already reaching for his phone. "I'll set up a private appointment at Neiman's. They'll bring options to us. No crowds, no waiting." And no chance of being seen shopping together like an actual couple.

She rolled her eyes. "Of course you'd make shopping into a power move."

"It saves time."

"It's pretentious."

"It's—" He stopped, gaze shifting over her shoulder. His stomach dropped as he recognized the two men heading their way. "They're here."

She turned as Knox and Gabriel approached. Knox's confident stride said he'd never been told no. Gabriel's relaxed gait said the world amused him. Both were smirking. Never a good sign.

"If we're finished, I'll go," she said.

"We haven't ordered."

"I'll let you enjoy your evening with the boys." She gathered her purse. "I'm going home to ramen and a glass of cheap wine. Text me the time for tomorrow."

She stood as the men reached the table. They exchanged confused glances as she prepared to leave. She nodded to both. "Gentlemen, the booth is all yours. Enjoy the evening."

Gabriel and Knox watched her go, then turned back to Ronan.

"What was that?" Gabriel asked. "Dinner meeting?"

"Strategy session."

Knox eyed him. "Since when do you have strategy sessions over dinner with your assistant?"

He exhaled. "Remember your brilliant suggestion about finding a 'family' for the Beauchamp deal?"

Understanding dawned on Knox's face. "No way. With her? And she agreed?"

"It's business. That's all." The skeptical glance they exchanged irritated him more than it should.

"Right. And that's why you couldn't keep your eyes off her as she walked away?" Gabriel's tone was the one he used to unsettle competitors.

"She's already on the payroll. She knows my schedule and how I work."

"The convenient choice," Knox said, leaning back with a smug look he'd always hated.

"Exactly. Convenience. Practicality." Ronan straightened his silverware, aligning the fork with the table's edge. "I know her. No need to bring in a stranger who might complicate things."

"Or someone you'd be less tempted by?" Gabriel asked.

"I'm not tempted by her. This is purely professional."

These two had known him too long. Saw too much. The air in the booth felt thinner.

"She's capable, professional, and completely uninterested in anything beyond this arrangement. And so am I."

Even as he spoke, he heard how defensive he sounded. The way Knox studied him suggested he was cataloging every tell.

Gabriel leaned forward, eyes gleaming with the instinct that made him lethal in negotiations. "Let's make this interesting. Since you're so sure this is all business, I bet you'll be the first one of us to fall."

He gave a short laugh, more habit than humor. "That's the dumbest bet I've ever heard."

Knox grinned. "Good. Then you won't mind putting your money where your mouth is."

Gabriel nodded. "If you fall for her, you owe us a weekend at your lake house. Fully stocked bar. No complaints."

Ronan rolled his eyes. "Fine. When I win, you both owe me a case of Macallan Twenty-Five."

They shook on it. Knox and Gabriel wore matching grins that made Ronan's skin prickle with unease.

It was the look they had before every major victory—like they knew a secret he didn't.

He acted like it was ridiculous. Like the idea of developing feelings for her didn't merit serious consideration.

But as the waiter arrived with menus, his thoughts slid back to the gala—the brush of his fingers at her back, the feel of her skin through thin fabric, the extra beat his hand had lingered when he helped her into the car. The surprising gentleness in her voice when she asked about his parents. He'd wanted to tell her more. To show her parts he'd kept hidden for years.

He couldn't help wondering about the bet. And if maybe he'd already lost.

Chapter 10

THE CLOCK on her computer screen barely moved. She glanced at the time again—4:47. Thirteen more minutes to wait before she could pretend she was leaving for an emergency dentist appointment, her shopping cover story.

She tapped her pen against the edge of her desk, trying to focus on an email she'd been attempting to finish for twenty minutes. The words blurred together.

"Are you ready?"

She startled at his voice and looked up to find Ronan standing by her desk, suit jacket already on, car keys in hand. Julia from Accounting, who'd been dropping off files, froze mid-motion.

"Yes," Devney said quickly, grabbing her purse and standing. She turned to Julia with an exaggerated sigh. "I was supposed to leave an hour ago, but you know the boss—he doesn't care much for other people's schedules." She gave him a pointed look, hoping Julia would buy the story. "He promised to get me to the dentist on time. I've got a toothache." She pointed to her right cheek.

Julia's curious expression relaxed into understanding.

"Good luck with the tooth," she said before heading back to her desk.

In the elevator his mouth twitched. "I care about things."

"Sure you do," she said. "Forecast models, profit margins, and properly aligned desk items."

"What was that about?" he asked as the doors closed.

"I saved us from being today's gossip on the office boards."

His forehead creased. "We have a gossip board?"

"Two, actually," she said. "The official one in the break room, and the unofficial Slack channel where everyone discusses everything from your ties to the disappearance of food from the communal fridge."

"We need to stop that," he muttered, as they reached the parking garage.

"Good luck. It's been around longer than I have." She slid into the passenger seat of his sleek car. "Besides, you'd have to fire half the accounting department."

He made a noncommittal sound as he pulled out of the garage, a noise that might have passed for agreement or mild tolerance.

The drive to Neiman Marcus was surprisingly comfortable. She watched the city blur past while a tight, nervous feeling grew in her stomach. Shopping with him, a man whose suits probably had their own insurance policy, promised to be an adventure.

When they arrived, he handed his keys to the valet with the casual confidence of someone who expected perfect service as a birthright. He navigated the store with purpose, ignoring the salespeople who bustled as he passed.

"Could you slow down? Some of us aren't built like gazelles."

He paused, glancing back to find her several paces behind. "Sorry," he said, actually waiting. "I'm used to moving at my pace."

"Yeah, I noticed," she said, catching up. "The Ronan Wilder special—everyone else's comfort be damned."

The corner of his mouth lifted. "Efficient."

They reached the personal-shopping floor, where a woman in an impeccable black dress approached. "Mr. Wilder," she said. "Perfect timing."

"Natalie will be with you momentarily," the woman said, leading them to a private suite that looked more like a luxury hotel room—plush chairs, a small table with champagne on ice, and an array of mirrors.

Natalie appeared—tall, elegant, and polished. "Mr. Wilder, how wonderful to see you again. And this must be…?"

"My fiancée," Ronan said. The word sent a tremor down Devney's spine. "As we discussed on the phone, she needs a full wardrobe for the weekend at the Beauchamps' estate. Something that fits the Vineyard."

"Of course. I've already pulled a selection based on the itinerary you sent over. They're waiting in the private suite." Natalie gestured toward a doorway draped in heavy velvet.

As they walked, Devney leaned closer to him, her voice a low murmur. "You sent an itinerary? And they already have clothes waiting?"

"Efficiency is expensive, Devney. That's why we're here."

Two long racks were already filled with silks, linens, and fine wools. Ronan settled into a leather armchair as if it were a throne. "Let's see if Natalie's eye matches mine."

The next hour became a blur. Ronan's critiques were immediate and maddeningly specific. "The sleeve length is wrong," he said about a cream blouse. "The color washes her out," he said about a camel-toned dress.

Eventually, Natalie smoothly pulled a breezy linen sundress in sea green from the rack. "Actually, for a casual luncheon on the terrace, this might be more the speed. Casual but elegant."

"That looks appropriately nautical," Devney said, touching the fabric.

"It's perfect," Ronan said, cutting in before Natalie could finish. His attention caught hers in the mirror, and something in his expression made her breath catch. "The color brings out your eyes."

Heat sparked through her as she took the dress to the dressing room. When she emerged, his reaction was subtle but unmistakable—his shoulders squared, his gaze sharpening.

"Well?" she said. "Am I Beauchamp-worthy yet?"

"It's acceptable," he said, though his eyes said more.

Natalie moved to the final section of the rack. "Now for the water activities. There will be swimming."

Natalie brought several options, all more elegant than Devney's faded one-piece at home. Devney hesitated, eyeing a navy one-piece with a plunging neckline. "I'll try them," she said, then added with a glance at him, "but you're not getting a preview."

His mouth curved. "You know I'm going to see it this weekend."

"That's different," she said quickly, heat blooming along her neck. "That's…situational."

She retreated and slipped it on. It felt more Vineyard than Malibu. Sophisticated. Polished. After a moment's hesitation, she wrapped herself in a plush robe and stepped out. "I'm getting this one," she said.

"We'll take it," Ronan told Natalie, "along with the sea-green sundress, the sailing outfit, the emerald gown, and…"—his gaze slid to Devney—"the swimsuit."

When she returned from changing, he was examining the swimsuit Natalie had laid out.

"Is it bad?"

He shook his head. "Not bad for the swimsuit. Bad for my concentration. You'll look perfect in it."

As she gathered her things, his attention drifted to her left hand and the sunflower ring.

"That thing is atrocious," he said. "I would never buy anything so garish."

"Until you pony up for a replacement that's new and real, this is what we've got. Besides, it has character."

He considered her for a long moment. "Noted. Are we done here?"

"Actually, I'm starving," she said. "But it's my turn to pick."

Thirty minutes later, he was staring at Tony's Pizzeria with visible dismay.

"You can't be serious."

"Absolutely serious," she said, pulling him through the door and directly to a booth at the back. "Tony's makes the best pizza in the city. Relax. No one here cares who you are or how much your watch costs."

Without thinking, she reached across the table, her fingers snagging the silk of his tie. As her knuckles grazed the warm skin of his throat, the muscle beneath her touch locked. He sat perfectly still, a sharp, sudden intensity taking hold as his dark gaze trapped hers.

"If you're going to sit in a pizza joint, at least try to look like you're not planning a hostile takeover."

"Devney." His voice was a low warning, but his mouth quirked at the corner as he met her eyes.

"Better. Now unbutton your collar."

With a resigned exhale, he obliged. A single undone button, a tiny rebellion, and somehow it made her heart thump harder. Seeing him a little undone felt unexpectedly intimate.

They clinked glasses of Chianti. "Tell me a truth," she said. "A detail I can use this weekend if conversation lags."

"I played cello. For years. I was quite good, actually."

"Ronan Wilder, a classical musician?"

"Is it that hard to believe?"

"No, actually. You have the hands for it. Long fingers." Heat crept up her neck as she realized she'd admitted to noticing his hands.

They traded small truths back and forth—his fondness for old black-and-white films, her quiet wish to matter to people who needed her. By the time they finished, she felt both relaxed and oddly energized. The night had turned more intimate than she'd imagined.

Outside, the evening air was cool against her flushed skin. "Thank you," she said. "For not hating my pizza place."

He looked down at her, his features softened by the street-light. "It was nice."

When they arrived at her apartment, he insisted on walking her to the door.

"I guess I'll see you tomorrow," she said. "At work. Where we're boss and assistant again."

"Yes," he said evenly. "Tomorrow."

He handed her the bags, their fingers brushing. The contact sparked—warmth racing up her arm. "Goodnight, Ronan."

"Goodnight, Devney."

She closed the door and leaned against it, wondering if he felt it too—this confusing connection, a bond formed over pizza, wine, and the kind of truths shared when guards are down.

Chapter 11

THE WEEK DRAGGED. Each day was an exercise in restraint as he watched the clock, counting down the hours until Friday arrived. Not because he was looking forward to a weekend with the Beauchamps—God, no—but because the anticipation itself felt like torture.

His office felt like a minefield; every interaction with her held a new, unspoken risk. Devney would breeze in with her usual sunflower energy, place coffee on his desk, and he'd notice things he'd successfully ignored for months—the small dimple that appeared in her left cheek when she fought a smile, the way her hands moved with grace when she explained details she cared about. It was maddening.

"Your 10:30 rescheduled," she said Thursday morning, leaning against his door frame with her tablet clutched to her chest. "And the quarterly projections are ready for review."

"Forward them to me."

"Already did," she said, and he could hear the eye roll in her voice without seeing it. "Also, Eleanor sent the final itinerary for the weekend."

That made him look up. "Anything we didn't expect?"

She nodded, one shoulder lifting in a casual gesture that somehow made his stomach tighten. "Apparently there's a sunset cocktail reception with some local politicians and business leaders tomorrow evening. The sailing outfit we bought should work for everything else, but Eleanor mentioned 'casual elegance' for the reception. Whatever that means."

"It means expensive clothing that's designed to look effortlessly thrown together," he said. "Which I happen to execute without fuss."

"Right," she said. "You have three blue ties that are the same."

"They're different shades."

"My point exactly." Her laughter filled his office, bright and unrestrained.

The noise messed with his pulse—offbeat and annoying as hell. That stupid bet with Knox and Gabriel tried to push its way in. He shut it down before it got comfortable.

"What time is the helicopter tomorrow?" he asked, changing the subject.

"Ten sharp. I'll meet you at the heliport at 9:30."

"I'll pick you up at 9," he said. "It'll be more convincing if we arrive together."

A moment of silence hung between them. "Right," she said. "The performance." She straightened, resuming her professional posture. "Nine it is. I'll be ready."

As she walked away, her words left a sharp ache inside him.

Friday morning was sharp and clear, the September sky an almost offensively perfect blue. He sat in his car outside Devney's apartment, checking his watch (9:01) and wondering why today of all days punctuality seemed to be a mystery to her. As he reached for his phone, her door flew open, and his breath caught.

She emerged in a cream-colored dress that floated around her knees, a light cardigan draped over her arm, her hair loose around her shoulders instead of pinned back in one of her usual work styles. She looked relaxed, radiant, and something in him stilled at the sight.

He stepped out of the car as she approached, taking her weekend bag from her without giving her a chance to object.

"You're late," he said, though she wasn't, not really.

"By one minute." She slid into the passenger seat as he held the door. "And you're uptight."

"I'm punctual," he said, closing her door with perhaps more force than necessary.

The drive to the heliport was subdued, their conversation limited to practical matters—the weather forecast, the anticipated arrival time, whether Andrew Beauchamp would grill him about financial projections over dinner. It felt safer this way, keeping to safe territory when everything else between them seemed suddenly charged.

The helicopter ride to Martha's Vineyard should have been quick and unremarkable. Instead, it became an exercise in self-control, the confined space shrinking around him with every breath she took beside him. When turbulence struck halfway through the journey, her hand found his arm, fingers curling around his wrist in an instinctive gesture. He felt the contact burn through the fabric of his shirt.

"Sorry," she said, removing her hand as quickly as she'd placed it. "Not a huge fan of flying."

He glanced at her, noting the slight pallor beneath her usual healthy glow. "You should have said something."

She shrugged. "And give you ammunition to tease me about? No thanks."

"I wouldn't have teased you.".

Her eyes met his, something unreadable in their amber depths. Neither of them spoke.

Then she smiled—a small, genuine curve of her lips that unsettled him. "Good to know."

The helicopter touched down on a private landing pad that overlooked the Atlantic. As the rotors slowed, a uniformed attendant opened the door and helped her step out onto the helipad. He followed, ducking his head beneath the still-spinning blades. Another staff member in crisp khakis and a navy polo with the Beauchamp crest approached to collect their bags.

"Welcome to Vineyard Haven," he said. "I'll take these to the main house for you."

Ronan nodded his thanks, surveying their surroundings as the helicopter powered down behind them. The Atlantic stretched out before them, vast and blue. The Beauchamp estate commanded prime real estate—an enormous white colonial mansion with black shutters, extensive gardens, and a path that led down to a private beach. An old-money establishment, built on generations of power, privilege, and strategic social moves.

"Holy mother of—" she said softly beside him, eyes wide. "This place is straight out of a movie."

He placed his hand on the small of her back, guiding her along the stone path toward the main house where Eleanor Beauchamp waited on the expansive porch, looking every inch the elegant hostess in white linen pants and a coral blouse. The light pressure of his palm against her back felt surprisingly right.

"Welcome, welcome!" Eleanor said, arms opening wide as they approached. "You made it in time for lunch."

"Eleanor," he said with a polite nod. "Thank you for having us."

"The pleasure is ours," she said, her gaze sliding to Deveney with obvious interest. "We rarely get to entertain young couples. Everyone our age is so dreadfully serious about everything."

Devney stepped forward. "Your home is stunning," she

said, gesturing to the gardens. "Those hydrangeas are magnificent."

Eleanor's face lit up. "Ah, you know your flowers."

"My grandmother was an avid gardener," she said. "She taught me everything about planting seasons, soil types, root systems—I was her little apprentice."

Eleanor hooked her arm through Devney's, leading her inside while launching into a detailed explanation of her gardening strategies. Ronan followed a step behind, feeling strangely like an afterthought as they disappeared into the foyer, their conversation about optimal soil pH already in full swing.

"Ronan," Andrew Beauchamp's deep voice came from the foyer as they entered. He stood at the foot of a sweeping staircase, looking both relaxed and imposing in tailored weekend attire.

"Good to see you."

"Andrew," he said, nodding in greeting as they shook hands. "Thank you for the invitation."

"We're delighted you could both make it," he said, his gaze drifting to where the women had paused by a massive flower arrangement. "Your fiancée is charming. Eleanor's already smitten."

He felt an unexpected surge of pride at Andrew's words. "She has that effect on people," he said, the truth of the statement hitting harder than he expected.

"Wilson will show you to your room," Andrew said, gesturing to a stoic older man who appeared silently at his side. "Get settled, then join us on the terrace for lunch."

Ronan nodded, glancing toward where their luggage had been placed near the foot of the sweeping staircase. "Room?" he asked, careful to keep his tone even. "Singular?"

Andrew looked at him. "Naturally," he said, his voice dry with a trace of humor. "Eleanor and I may value tradition,

Ronan, but we're hardly Victorian. You're engaged to be married—we wouldn't dream of separating you."

Heat crawled up the back of his neck—a sensation he hadn't felt since his early twenties. He wasn't embarrassed by the implication; he was unsettled by how his mind conjured images of her in a shared bed, her hair spilled across pillows meant for two.

"This way, sir," Wilson said, already moving toward the stairs.

Ronan caught Devney's eye across the foyer and gave a slight tilt of his head, indicating she should follow. She excused herself from Eleanor and joined him, her questioning look turning to confusion as Wilson led them up the massive staircase.

"Our room," he said as they climbed. "Singular."

"As in one?" she said softly, eyes widening.

He nodded.

"The Rose Suite," Wilson said, pushing the doors open with reverence.

The room beyond was beautiful—spacious, with high ceilings, cream-colored walls, and accents of rose throughout. Sunlight poured through tall windows that overlooked the ocean, illuminating a king-sized four-poster bed draped in luxurious linens, a sitting area with a fireplace, and double doors leading to what he assumed was an en-suite bathroom.

It was elegant, refined, and romantic—a room designed for lovers to retreat from the world.

And there was, indeed, only one bed.

"Wow," she said softly, her voice full of awe as she stepped inside. "This is gorgeous."

Wilson nodded, pleased by her reaction. "Mrs. Beauchamp selected it personally for you.

She thought you might appreciate the view."

"It's perfect," she said, moving toward the windows. "Thank you, Wilson."

He bowed. "Lunch will be served on the east terrace in thirty minutes. May I show you the way?"

"We'll find it," Ronan said, noting their luggage had been placed discreetly near the expansive wardrobe.

Wilson nodded and withdrew, closing the doors behind him with a click that seemed to seal their fate.

The moment they were alone, she turned to him, her composed facade slipping. "One bed," she said, stating the obvious.

"I see that," he said, surveying the room more thoroughly. A small sofa sat in the bedroom—elegant but impractical for sleeping. Only five feet long, it seemed laughable compared to his height of well over six feet.

"You won't fit on that," she said, following his gaze to the sofa. "Not unless you remove your legs."

"I'll manage," he said, unbuttoning his suit jacket and hanging it in the wardrobe to avoid wrinkles. "It's only for two nights."

She bit her lip, a gesture he was recognizing as a sign of genuine concern rather than her usual teasing. "We could alternate," she said. "I'll take the couch tonight. You take it tomorrow."

He gave her a look that made it clear what he thought of that idea.

"Fine," she sighed, running a hand through her hair. "Be chivalrous and uncomfortable. Don't complain when you can't stand up straight on Monday."

He focused on unpacking his essentials. "We should head down for lunch," he said, checking his watch. "They'll be expecting us."

She nodded, disappearing into the bathroom to freshen up. When she emerged, she'd applied a touch of lip gloss and brushed her hair. The sight altered his heart rate in surprising ways.

"Ready, fiancé?" she asked, holding out her hand. Her eyes sparkled with teasing affection, even as her fingers trembled, betraying the nerves beneath her confidence.

He took her hand—small and trembling but stilling the moment it met his. "Ready."

Lunch was an elaborate affair served on fine china beneath a white pergola draped with climbing roses. The conversation flowed with surprising ease, primarily because of her natural ability to charm and engage. She asked intelligent questions about Andrew's newest investments, laughed at Eleanor's stories about local politics, and somehow made him appear more human by association.

"So, Devney," Eleanor said over dessert, a delicate panna cotta topped with fresh berries. "What was your first impression of Ronan? He can be rather intimidating, I imagine."

Devney's eyes met his across the table, lit with mischief.

"Terrifying," she said with a laugh. "I spilled coffee on my résumé during the interview and was convinced he'd throw me out on the spot."

"Did you?" Eleanor asked him, clearly amused.

"The résumé was still legible," he said, finding himself grinning at the memory. "And her qualifications were impressive enough to overlook the coffee stains."

"Plus," Devney said, "I think he was amused by how badly I was trying to pretend it hadn't happened."

"I could see your hands shaking," he said, the detail surfacing from a memory he hadn't realized he'd stored. "But you answered every question despite it."

She stared at him. "You never told me that."

"You never asked," he said simply.

Eleanor watched with obvious satisfaction. "When did you

realize it was more than work?" she asked, glancing between them.

The question hung in the air, deceptively simple, yet loaded with danger. This was the heart of their charade—the moment their story had to sound real.

"I knew after the Morris acquisition," he said before she could speak, surprising himself with the certainty in his voice. "We worked through the night on the final contract details.

"Around four in the morning, when most people would have been complaining or making mistakes, she was still sharp, still challenging my assumptions, still improving the terms."

Devney's eyes widened, but he kept speaking, unable to stop now that he'd started.

"She fell asleep at her desk before dawn," he said, the memory startlingly vivid, "her head on a stack of contracts, pen still in her hand. And I realized I'd met no one so stubbornly determined, so brilliantly persistent. A person who pushed back against my worst tendencies instead of accommodating them."

The table had gone silent, everyone watching him with curious expressions. He cleared his throat, suddenly aware that he'd revealed more than he'd intended. "That's when I knew she was different," he said, reaching for his water glass to occupy his hands.

"How romantic," Eleanor sighed, clearly delighted by this revelation.

Devney's gaze remained fixed on him, an unreadable expression on her face. "I didn't know you remembered that night," she said.

"I remember everything," he said.

A moment of charged silence followed, broken only when Andrew suggested they take a walk along the beach before dinner. Eleanor seconded the idea, rising from her chair.

"Wonderful plan," she said. "The fresh air will do us all good."

As they filed toward the path leading to the beach, Devney fell into step beside Ronan, her voice low enough that only he could hear.

"That was quite a performance," she said.

"It wasn't entirely a performance," he replied, the words feeling like stones dragged from

deep within him.

She looked up at him then, her expression open and vulnerable, and the look made him stop, unable to move for a moment. Across the garden, Eleanor called her name, beckoning her

forward to continue their earlier conversation about hydrangeas.

He watched her go, wondering when the difference between the lie and the truth had

gotten so hard to see.

The afternoon passed in a succession of polite activities—the beach walk, a tour of Andrew's wine cellar, and finally retreating to their room to dress for dinner. She disappeared into the bathroom with her garment bag, leaving him to change in the bedroom. He was adjusting his cufflinks when she emerged, and the sight of her made his fingers still.

She wore the blue dress they'd purchased at Neiman's. The fabric draped well over her curves, and the color intensified the unique shade of her eyes. Her hair was swept up into an elegant knot, revealing the graceful line of her neck and shoulders.

"Will I do?" she asked, like she wasn't sure of the answer.

"You're beautiful," he said, the words emerging rougher than intended.

A flush spread across her cheeks, delicate and genuine. "Thank you," she said. "You clean up nicely yourself."

Dinner was a formal affair, with several other couples from the Beauchamps' social circle joining them in the grand dining room. Devney navigated the complex social dynamics with surprising grace, charming the venture capitalist seated to her left while holding her own in a debate about sustainable investment with a retired professor across the table.

Despite all the conversations going on around him, he found himself watching her, struck by how she fit into this world she'd had no reason to belong in—but somehow did. She spoke with confidence but without pretension, laughed without restraint, and somehow made everyone around her feel valued.

Eleanor noticed his attention, leaning closer as the dessert course was being served. "She's remarkable," she said. "Quite charming. And clearly very much in love with you."

"Yes," he said simply, because denying it seemed impossible. "She is remarkable."

By the time they retreated to their room after dinner, exhaustion had settled deep in his bones—not from the activities of the day, but from the constant vigilance required to maintain their charade while fighting his own increasingly conflicted feelings.

"I'll change in the bathroom," she said, gathering her things. "Give you a chance to get comfortable on your miniature couch."

He nodded, already removing his tie and unbuttoning his collar. The moment the bathroom door closed behind her, he sank onto the edge of the sofa, running a hand over his face. This weekend promised more challenges than he'd anticipated —and none of them were the ones he'd prepared for.

After the contract was signed, this charade would end. They could go back to their normal roles, their comfortable professional distance. A few more days of pretending. The thought should have brought relief. Instead, it left an emptiness inside him. The problem has changed. It wasn't convincing the Beauchamps that they were engaged. The problem was remembering that they weren't.

He changed quickly into sleep pants and a T-shirt, then surveyed the sofa with grim determination. It was, as she had pointed out, at least a foot too short for his frame. Still, he'd endured worse discomfort for business purposes.

He was arranging a spare blanket and pillow when the bathroom door opened. He turned,

expecting to see her in sensible pajamas and felt his heart stop.

She stood in the doorway, hair loose around her shoulders, wearing what could only be described as a sleep shirt—though *shirt* was generous, given how little of her it covered. The material barely reached mid-thigh, revealing the unexpected length of her tanned legs.

Tiny, embroidered sunflowers dotted the pale-yellow fabric, a whimsical touch that somehow made the entire vision more devastating.

"Sorry," she said, noticing his stare. "I didn't pack anything else. I wasn't planning to

share a room."

"It's fine," he said, the words emerging strangled.

She crossed to the bed, tugging the hem of her sleep shirt enough to make his mouth go dry. "Are you sure you don't want to share?" she asked, gesturing to the king-sized expanse. "There's plenty of room. We could put pillows between us or something."

"I'm sure," he said, more forcefully than necessary. The thought of lying next to her all night, separated only by decorative pillows, was a form of torture he wasn't prepared to endure.

She shrugged, moving with a grace that pulled tension tight

inside him. "Your funeral," she said, settling against the pillows. "Or at least your spine's."

He turned away, focusing on making the sofa as tolerable as possible. When he glanced back, she'd turned off her bedside lamp, her form a gentle curve beneath the luxurious bedding.

"Goodnight, Ronan," she said into the darkness.

"Goodnight, Devney," he said, lowering himself onto the too-small sofa with a sense of grim resignation.

As he curled into what could only be described as a fetal position to fit his frame onto the inadequate furniture, one thought circled relentlessly through his mind. *Kill me now.*

Chapter 12

SHE WOKE to the sound of his phone alarm, followed by a muffled curse that pulled a laugh from her as she buried her face deeper into the pillow. Propping herself up on one elbow, she peered over the edge of the absurdly comfortable king-sized bed and spotted her fake fiancé twisted on the sofa like a human pretzel. One foot dangled off the armrest, and his neck was bent at an angle that all but guaranteed a future filled with chiropractor visits and regret.

"Sleep well?" she asked.

His gaze slid to hers, a mixture of irritation and heat that curled low in her stomach. "Splendidly," he said, his voice thick with sleep. "Nothing like spending the night folded like origami."

After quick showers and changing into their sailing outfits, they joined the Beauchamps on the veranda for breakfast. Eleanor and Andrew were already seated, looking effortlessly elegant despite the early hour.

"Did you sleep well?" Eleanor asked as they sat down.

"Like a dream," Devney said truthfully, then caught

Ronan's subtle wince as he adjusted his position. "The Rose Suite is beautiful."

An hour later, they were aboard the *Tidewater*—a sleek, gleaming vessel that Andrew described as a "modest day sail-boat," but looked to her like it belonged on the cover of a yachting magazine. The morning was perfect for sailing, with clear skies and a gentle breeze that carried them across the glittering water of Vineyard Sound.

The most remarkable thing was watching Ronan move with confidence across the deck when Andrew called him over to help with the sails. His hands worked the ropes and rigging with ease, revealing yet another layer to the man she thought she knew so well.

"He's quite good," Eleanor said, following her gaze. "Andrew doesn't ask for help unless someone actually knows what they're doing."

"He never ceases to amaze me," she said.

"Would you like Andrew to take a photo of you two?" Eleanor asked, as they rounded a beautiful stretch of coastline. "The lighting is perfect."

The words caught in her throat as Eleanor turned, already calling Andrew over with her idea. Ronan appeared behind them, his expression blank.

"I'm terrible in photos," she said softly to him.

"Impossible," he said, his hand finding the small of her back—a gesture that was becoming second nature. His palm pressed against her thin top, sending a quick tremor through her.

Following Andrew's direction, she moved to the railing and turned toward the view, extending her arms outward in the classic "king of the world" pose. She felt both silly and exhilarated, with his hands settling on her waist from behind.

"Beautiful!" Andrew said. "One more!"

What happened next seemed to unfold in slow motion. A

sudden wave caught the boat, causing it to lurch sharply. She felt herself losing balance, her outstretched position leaving her with nothing to grab. His hands tightened instinctively around her waist, but the sudden movement had already sent her pitching forward.

For one suspended moment, she was aware of his grip slipping, Eleanor's gasp, and the sickening realization that she was going overboard. Then she was falling, a dizzying view of blue sky, then the sudden, cold impact of the water.

She surfaced spluttering, pushing wet hair from her eyes in time to see a clean, arcing dive as Ronan entered the water barely five feet away from her.

He surfaced with powerful strokes, reaching her in seconds. "Are you hurt?"

"Only my dignity," she said, still trying to process what had happened. "I didn't expect an impromptu swim today."

Relief passed over his face. "Next time, warn me before you decide to go for a dip," he said, one arm sliding around her waist to keep her afloat.

The *Tidewater* had continued moving after their fall, leaving them perhaps thirty yards away—close enough to see Eleanor's concerned expression, but far enough that they had a moment of unexpected privacy in Vineyard Sound.

"Are you really okay?" he asked, his arm still secure around her.

She nodded, suddenly aware of their proximity—his face inches from hers, water droplets clinging to his eyelashes, his normally perfect hair slicked back from his forehead. "My hero," she said, trying for levity but hearing the breathless quality in her voice.

His features grew more intense, his eyes moving from hers to her lips and back again. For a breathless moment, she thought he might kiss her—right there in the Atlantic.

The approach of the *Tidewater* broke the moment, Andrew

calling instructions and Eleanor extending boat hooks for them to grab. His arm released her as they both reached for the hooks, allowing Andrew and Eleanor to help them back aboard.

"I am so sorry," Eleanor said, her tone fussy, wrapping a fluffy towel around Devney's shoulders. "That wave came out of nowhere."

"Entirely my fault," Devney said, reassuring her, teeth chattering despite the warm air. "I was showing off with that pose."

"We should head back so you both can change," Eleanor said. "We have lunch reservations at the yacht club at one."

Back at the house, they were ushered upstairs with instructions to shower and change. The moment their bedroom door closed, the tension that had been building since their water rescue intensified.

"You should shower first," he said, already moving toward his suitcase. "You were in the water longer."

"Are we not going to talk about what happened?" she asked, surprising herself with her directness.

He paused, his back to her. "You fell. I jumped in after you. There's nothing to discuss."

"Right," she said, ignoring the sharp ache of disappointment. "Nothing at all."

She retreated to the bathroom, letting the hot water wash away the salt and the uncomfortable feeling that she was reading far too much into every interaction between them.

THE VINEYARD HAVEN Yacht Club was as exclusive as she'd imagined, with weathered shingle siding, gleaming wood floors, and walls covered in nautical memorabilia. They were seated at a prime table overlooking the harbor, where sailboats bobbed in the midday sun.

Lunch proceeded pleasantly, with conversation flowing between business topics and more personal matters. She was in the middle of describing her grandmother's blueberry pie recipe to Eleanor when a recognizable piano melody drifted from the far corner of the dining room.

"They've started the afternoon music," Eleanor said with pleasure. "The club has a small ensemble on weekends."

"They're quite good," Devney said, recognizing the piece. "Though I bet Ronan could give their cellist a run for his money."

The words slipped out before she had the chance to stop them. His head snapped up, his eyes meeting hers with a mixture of shock and something that might have been betrayal.

"You play the cello?" Eleanor asked, clearly delighted by this revelation. "What a wonderful discovery!"

His jaw tightened. "I used to," he said, his tone dismissive. "A long time ago."

"He's being modest," she said, unable to stop herself. "He still plays. And he's incredible."

"How wonderful," Eleanor said. "We have a beautiful cello at the house—it was my father's. No one's played it in years, but it's kept in perfect condition."

"I don't play publicly," he said firmly, giving Devney a look that clearly communicated she should drop the subject.

"He played for me on our third date," she said, the lie coming easily. "Bach's 'Cello Suite No. 1.' I cried, it was so beautiful."

"You simply must play for us this evening," Eleanor said. "Before the cocktail reception."

His expression remained neutral, but she could feel his tension from across the table. "I'm afraid I'm out of practice," he said.

Eleanor's attention sharpened. Retreat would look like weakness.

Devney stepped in before the silence could be used against him.

"I've heard you practice at home," she said, smiling, her hand finding his. "You played last week."

His fingers tensed beneath hers, but he didn't pull away. Instead, he turned his hand to capture hers, his grip tight enough to convey his irritation.

"Perhaps a brief piece," he said, though the lightness in his tone didn't quite match the tension in his eyes.

When they returned to the house after lunch, he disappeared to make work calls while she spent the afternoon with Eleanor, touring her impressive art collection. Soon it was time to prepare for the evening's cocktail reception.

Back in their room, she found him halfway dressed in tailored navy pants and a crisp white shirt.

"I laid out your 'casual elegance' option," he said, nodding toward the bed where a simple but elegant cocktail dress in deep emerald hung waiting.

"Thank you," she said, touched by the gesture despite his obvious lingering irritation. "Though I'm not sure you're speaking to me at the moment."

He finished with one cufflink before looking up. "Why did you tell them I play the cello?"

"Because you do," she said simply. "And it's one of the most genuine things about you."

"What does that mean?" he asked.

"I think there's more to you than you let people see."

He studied her for a moment, the silence between them thick with unspoken thoughts. Finally, he gave a single nod.

"I'll play one piece," he said. "For the sake of our cover story."

By the time she emerged from the bathroom, hair styled

and makeup freshened, he was waiting by the door, handsome in the navy pants now paired with a light gray blazer over the white shirt.

"You look beautiful," he said, his eyes moving appreciatively over the emerald dress.

"So do you," she said, and something in his face eased—vulnerable, real. It sent a ripple through her she wasn't prepared for.

They made their way downstairs to find Eleanor waiting in the library, a magnificent room with floor-to-ceiling bookshelves and a grand piano in one corner. Beside it stood a cello on a stand, its wood gleaming with the deep patina that comes only from age and care.

"My father's pride and joy," Eleanor said, following his gaze to the instrument. "A French cello from the late 1800s."

He approached it with visible reverence, his fingers hovering above the wood. "It's exquisite," he said, and she glimpsed the man beneath the carefully constructed exterior.

"Please," Eleanor said. "Feel free to examine it more closely."

After a moment's hesitation, he gently lifted the cello, his hands steady as he positioned it and took the bow Eleanor offered.

He sat on the edge of a nearby chair, the instrument settling into place. His back straightened, his shoulders eased, and something in his eyes softened.

Andrew appeared in the doorway, nodding approvingly. "Excellent," he said. "We're in for a treat, it seems."

Ronan's eyes met Devney's across the room. She gave him a reassuring look, hoping he could see how much this glimpse of his hidden self meant to her.

He took a moment to pluck each string, the low, resonant notes vibrating through the quiet library. Finding them flat from years of silence, he adjusted the pegs with practiced, steady fingers, his ear tilted toward the wood until the pitch was perfect. Only when the instrument was finally brought back to life did he position the bow, close his eyes briefly, and play.

The melody filled the room, alive and flowing, each note connecting with grace.

Watching him was mesmerizing—the subtle changes in his expression as he navigated emotional passages, the confident movement of his fingers along the neck of the cello, the way his entire body seemed to exist in perfect harmony with the instrument. This was him stripped of his armor, vulnerable, and powerful in a different way than she was accustomed to seeing him.

When the last note faded, there was perfect silence, as if none of them dared to be the first to break the spell he'd cast.

Then Andrew applauded, followed quickly by Eleanor, their appreciation clear in their faces. She remained still, unable to look away from him as he opened his eyes, seeming to return from some place distant and private.

His gaze found hers, something settling in his features—relief, maybe, or something close to peace.

She didn't applaud. It would've felt wrong, too performative for a performance that had felt so personal.

Instead, she looked at him, hoping he could read in her face what she couldn't quite put into words: that she saw him—really saw him—for perhaps the first time.

"That was extraordinary," Eleanor said, genuine emotion in her voice. "Truly beautiful."

He returned the cello to its stand. "The instrument deserves the credit. It's exceptional."

"Nonsense," Andrew said. "The finest instrument in the world is nothing without the right hands to play it."

As they moved from the library toward the terrace where the cocktail reception would be held, his hand found the small of her back again—that increasingly natural gesture that somehow felt both possessive and protective. But this time, his touch lingered, his fingers tracing a small circle against the fabric of her dress before settling into their usual pressure.

As they stepped onto the terrace, he leaned close, his breath against her ear.

"Thank you," he said.

"For what?" she asked, turning to meet his gaze.

He held her eyes, steady and unblinking.

"For seeing me," he said.

She didn't get the chance to respond—Eleanor was already calling them over to discuss the guest list, and the moment was gone. But as they moved into their roles for the evening—the happy, engaged couple among the Beauchamps' distinguished guests—she couldn't ignore her trembling hands or the sudden warmth that spread through her with each of his glances.

What terrified her most wasn't the performance they were giving for the Beauchamps and their friends. It was the possibility that when Monday came and they returned to real life, she might not stop herself from wanting what wasn't actually hers to keep.

____

Chapter 13

____

THE RECEPTION DRAGGED PAST ELEVEN, each conversation blending into the next as he tracked her movements across the terrace. Business leaders from all over the Northeast discussed market projections and vacation properties, while she made even the notoriously difficult wife of the Massachusetts senator laugh within minutes of meeting her.

When the last guest finally departed, they climbed the stairs to their room in exhausted silence. An ache had settled at the base of his skull during the final hour, and his throat felt raw despite barely speaking above the ambient noise.

"Your turn for the bed," she said, already pulling pillows from the massive king-sized mattress. "I'm taking the sofa tonight."

"No." The word came out sharper than intended.

She paused, arms full of bedding. "We agreed to alternate."

"I never agreed to that." He moved toward his suitcase, avoiding her gaze. "I'll take the sofa again."

Her exasperation was palpable. "Your stubbornness is going to have serious consequences for your spine."

But he'd already made the decision. The way she'd said it, like she owed him a debt for his discomfort, didn't sit right. Some outdated sense of chivalry, perhaps. Or respect for how much she'd need to juggle Monday morning while he'd cleared his schedule for the Beauchamp contract.

She disappeared into the bathroom, and he arranged himself on the inadequate sofa, trying to find a position that wouldn't leave him crippled by morning. Sleep eluded him. The combination of Bach still humming through his veins and the furniture's dimensions guaranteed that. His limbs ached from the unnatural angles, but another discomfort lurked beneath the physical strain: a heaviness in his muscles that felt different from mere exhaustion.

He dismissed it. A night of poor sleep. The sudden swim in cold Atlantic water. The strain of maintaining their charade.

Hours passed. The ache at the base of his skull intensified, and chills began running through him despite the room's warmth. His body was betraying him after years of disciplined control over every aspect of his existence. The irony cut deep: the man who prided himself on never showing weakness was falling apart in front of the one person whose opinion had begun to matter more than it should.

He glanced toward the bed where she slept, her hair spread across the pillows, one hand tucked beneath her cheek. The sight created a longing so sharp it cut through even the fever's haze. Not just physical desire, though that was undeniably present, but a deeper need he didn't know how to name. The urge to slide under those covers beside her, to feel the heat of her body against the strange coldness that had seeped into his bones.

By the gray pre-dawn, his condition had worsened. He stood, swaying as dizziness swept over him. The bathroom mirror confirmed his suspicions: dark circles underscored his eyes, and an unusual pallor had settled beneath his tan. He splashed cold water on his face and swallowed two aspirin from his travel kit, knowing they wouldn't be enough but clinging to the illusion of control they provided.

Control. The word mocked him as another chill rattled through his frame.

When she stirred hours later, he had showered, dressed, and forced himself into a passable imitation of normal. The aspirin had dulled the headache to a manageable throb, though his limbs felt oddly heavy.

"Morning," she said, stretching beneath the covers. Her eyes narrowed as she studied him. "You look terrible."

"Your morning compliments never fail to charm."

She sat up, concern replacing sleepiness. "Are you okay?"

"I'm fine." He turned toward his suitcase to avoid her scrutiny. "I'm eager to get out of here and back to real life."

The words felt like a betrayal even as he spoke them. This weekend, this version of himself he'd discovered in her presence, felt more real than anything he'd experienced in years.

"Right." Her tone suggested she didn't believe him. "Back to reality."

She slipped into the bathroom without waiting for a reply, leaving him with the unsettling sense that his facade hadn't fooled her at all.

Brunch was an elaborate affair spread across the Beauchamps' solarium. He pushed food around his plate while Eleanor shared stories about her father's art collection and Andrew outlined the final steps for their merger.

"Wednesday works," he said, when Andrew mentioned the paperwork timeline, forcing himself to take a sip of coffee that tasted metallic on his tongue.

By the time they prepared to leave, his headache had returned

The helicopter waited, rotors already spinning. He reached for her hand to guide her toward it, the gesture instinctive rather than rehearsed. Her fingers curled into his like they'd done it a thousand times.

Once inside, the doors sealed, and the world became a thrum of sound. He slipped on the headset, adjusting the mic as the rotors roared overhead. Across from him, she did the same. He leaned back against the seat and closed his eyes as they lifted off. The motion sent his stomach lurching in protest.

"Ronan?" Her voice came through the headset, concern clear even through the tinny audio. "You're shivering."

He opened his eyes to find her watching him, her face creased with worry. "It's cold," he said, which wasn't entirely a lie. Despite the mild September day, he felt frozen from the inside out.

"It's seventy-five degrees," she said, reaching across to press her palm against his forehead. The gesture was so surprising, so intimate, that he didn't think to pull away. Her hand was cool against his burning skin, and for a moment the relief was so profound he nearly groaned aloud.

"You're burning up," she said, her voice sharp with alarm.

"I'm fine," he said.

"You are not fine. You're sick."

"I don't get sick."

She rolled her eyes, somehow both exasperated and fond. "Congratulations on being human after all. When was the last time you took anything for that fever?"

He checked his watch, startled to realize how much time had passed. "Aspirin at six. Wore off."

She dug through her purse, producing a small travel container. "Tylenol. Take two."

He swallowed the pills with water from the bottle she offered, then leaned back again, surrendering to the exhaustion that threatened to pull him under.

"It's the swim," she said through the headset. "Cold water, stress, not enough sleep on that ridiculous sofa. Your immune system didn't stand a chance."

"Worth it," he said, the words slipping out without conscious thought.

"What was?" she asked.

He opened his eyes to find her watching him with a mixture of concern and uncertainty. The fever had lowered his defenses, made him reckless with truths he normally kept locked away.

"Jumping in after you," he said, too drained to filter his thoughts. "Would do it again."

Something flashed across her face, wonder and warmth that made his chest tighten.

"Who knew you had a knight in shining armor hiding under all those tailored suits," she said, the teasing note failing to mask the genuine emotion threading through her voice.

The rest of the flight passed in a haze. They landed at the Manhattan heliport. He managed to get out, but when he reached for his weekend bag, she intercepted him, slinging both bags over her shoulder with surprising strength.

"Keys," she said firmly, holding out her hand.

"Why?" The word came out slurred, his tongue feeling thick and uncooperative.

"Give me your car keys. You aren't driving," she said, leaving no room for argument. "I'm driving."

Nobody drove his car. The world tilted dangerously, and he had to close his eyes until it steadied.

"I can get a car service."

"Don't be ridiculous." She maneuvered them toward the parking area where he'd left his car on Friday. "Keys. Now."

He surrendered them, too miserable to maintain his usual iron grip on control. She helped him into the passenger seat with quiet competence before stowing their bags in the trunk.

When she slid into the driver's seat, she adjusted everything, as if she'd been driving his car for years.

"Your address?" she asked, starting the engine.

"You don't need to come home with me."

She gave him a sidelong glance as she pulled out of the parking space. "Address, please."

"Devney," he said, summoning what little energy he had left for an argument, "the weekend is over. Contract nearly signed. You're off duty."

Her hands tightened on the steering wheel, knuckles going white. "Is that what you think this is? A duty?"

"It's a business arrangement," he said, though every instinct rebelled against the words. "Consider yourself released from further obligations."

She pulled the car to an abrupt stop at a red light, turning to face him with fire in her eyes. "For a brilliant businessman, you can be remarkably dense."

"Why?"

"A business partner would leave you at the curb with your keys and a polite 'take care.' A colleague might call a car and send a follow-up email on Monday. But someone who cares about you wouldn't walk away when you're clearly not okay," she said. "Give me the address and let me help you."

"890 Park Avenue," he said after a moment, surrendering to whatever this was between them. "Penthouse B."

She nodded, making a skillful turn uptown. "Thank you."

They drove in relative silence, the classical music playing through the car's speakers. Bach again, he realized with bitter irony. The same piece he'd played for her yesterday, when the world had felt different and his defenses hadn't been quite so compromised.

"You don't have to take care of me," he said finally, unable to leave the matter unsettled. "I can manage."

She sighed. "I know you can manage. You've probably been managing everything alone since you were twelve. But sometimes, the point isn't whether you can do everything by yourself. It's whether you should have to."

"I don't need—" he began, but she cut him off.

"Need is irrelevant," she said simply. "Want, on the other hand…"

She navigated through the Sunday traffic, handling his car with surprising skill. He leaned his head against the cool window, closing his eyes against another wave of dizziness.

"For what it's worth," she added quietly, "I want to help. Not because of our arrangement. Not because it's good for business. Simply because."

Because she cared. As if caring could be that simple, uncomplicated by expectations or obligations or the careful cost-benefit analyses that governed every other relationship in his life.

By the time they reached his building, speaking required more energy than he possessed. She handled everything: valeting the car, retrieving their bags, nodding to the doorman with such confidence that he didn't question her presence at Ronan's side.

In the elevator, she supported more of his weight than he wanted to admit, her arm firm around his waist as his fever climbed higher. The short walk from the elevator to his door felt interminable.

"Which key?" she asked softly, holding up the ring.

"The black fob."

She unlocked the door and helped him inside. His apartment looked strange through feverish eyes: too large, too sterile, too empty.

This was his life, he realized with uncomfortable clarity. Beautiful, expensive, and utterly devoid of warmth.

"Bedroom?" she asked, still supporting him as they crossed the threshold.

He nodded toward the hallway to the right, letting her guide him down it. His bedroom appeared before them, the massive bed with its hospital corners and dark bedding suddenly the most inviting sight imaginable.

"Sit," she said, lowering him to the edge of the mattress with careful hands.

He wanted to protest as she knelt before him, her fingers working to untie his shoes. This level of intimacy crossed boundaries.

The sight of her there, kneeling at his feet, struck him as profoundly wrong and strangely right simultaneously.

She set his shoes aside with care before helping him swing his legs onto the bed. The domesticity of the gesture felt both foreign and familiar, as if they'd done this a hundred times before.

"Rest," she said, pulling the covers over him with gentle hands. "I'll get water and more Tylenol."

As she turned to leave, he caught her wrist, his fingers circling the delicate bones. The touch was electric, even through the haze of fever.

"Why?" he asked, the single word carrying the weight of everything he couldn't voice.

She looked down at where his hand held hers, then back to his face. "Because I've spent six months watching you take care of everyone else. The company. Your clients. Your team. Even me, in your own prickly way." Her lips curved. "It's time someone took care of *you* for a change."

He released her wrist, watching as she walked to the door.

She paused at the threshold and glanced back. "Besides," she said, "your refrigerator is probably stocked with nothing but protein shakes and one sad apple. Someone needs to order you real food."

With that, she disappeared down the hallway, leaving him alone with the realization that for the first time in years, he'd willingly let someone cross the fortified boundaries of his private life.

More unsettling still was the recognition that instead of regretting it, he found himself hoping she'd stay.

Chapter 14

SHE SLIPPED OUT of his bedroom, determined to find something to relieve his fever. His bathroom was what she'd expected—immaculate, expensive, and organized with exacting care. The medicine cabinet yielded Tylenol, which she grabbed before filling a glass with cool water.

When she returned to his bedroom, his normally composed features were flushed, dark hair falling across his forehead. Disheveled, vulnerable, and nothing like the version of him she was used to seeing.

"Here," she said, perching on the edge of the bed. "You need to take these and drink all of this water."

He struggled to sit up, and she instinctively slid an arm behind his shoulders to help. The heat from his skin, even through his shirt, was alarming.

"You're still burning up," she said quietly, pressing her palm to his forehead again. "We should check your temperature. Where's your thermometer?"

"Medicine cabinet. Top shelf."

She found the thermometer just where he'd said it would be, of course.

When she returned, he had sunk back against the pillows, his eyes closed.

"Ronan," she said. "I'm going to take your temperature now."

His eyes opened, an eyebrow arching weakly. "Not very romantic."

A startled laugh escaped her. "Are you delirious already? Because you making jokes is definitely a symptom."

His thermometer was a sleek digital model that looked like it belonged in a doctor's office. She pointed it at his temple and pressed the button.

The device beeped within seconds. She read the display, eyes widening.

"103.2," she said. "That's not good. You need a doctor."

"I'll be fine," he said, though his voice lacked its usual authority.

"Okay," she said, fixing him with a stern look. "But if this doesn't bring your fever down, I'm calling someone. Non-negotiable."

He sighed, too exhausted to argue. "Fine. Acceptable terms."

She headed to his kitchen to get what she needed for a compress. The space was sleek, spotless, and looked barely used—exactly what she'd expected from him.

She filled a bowl with ice and water, grabbed a clean dish towel, and returned to find him shivering beneath the covers.

"Cold," he whispered, pulling the duvet tighter around himself.

"I know," she said, setting the bowl on his nightstand. "But we need to cool you down." She soaked the towel, wrung it out, and placed it on his forehead. He flinched at the contact. "Sorry. Necessary evil."

For the next hour, she replaced the cold cloth each time it lost its chill, watching with growing concern as his shivering intensified despite the fever-reducer. His usually calm face was tight with discomfort. He mumbled about quarterly reports and contracts—a detail that might have been funny any other time.

When his temperature refused to drop below 103, she hesitated, weighing her options. She'd cared for her grandmother through several winter illnesses, and she remembered what the doctor had recommended when conventional methods weren't working. Though it seemed counterintuitive with his high fever, sometimes comfort was what the body needed most to heal.

"Ronan," she said, shaking his shoulder gently. "You're still shivering too much. The cold compresses aren't helping if you can't relax."

His eyes opened to half-mast. "What else…?"

She hesitated, searching for the right words. "Sometimes contact helps," she said, trying to sound clinical rather than mortified. "Not to heat you up more—your body's already doing that—but to help you feel less miserable while the medicine works."

Even in his feverish state, his eyebrows rose. "You're suggesting…?"

"Don't make this weird," she said, kicking off her shoes. "I'm going to sit with you until you stop shaking. That's it."

A ghost of his usual smirk appeared. "Shouldn't it be skin-to-skin contact?"

She snorted, grateful for the moment of levity. "In your dreams, Wilder."

"Yes," he said quietly, his gaze direct despite the fever. "You have been."

She drew a sharp breath. His eyes held a raw honesty brought on by the fever, a look that made her own heart pound.

"That's definitely the delirium talking," she managed,

keeping her tone casual even as warmth and recklessness threatened to surface.

"Perhaps," he said, eyelids heavy.

She circled to the other side of the bed and sat beside him, her back against the headboard.

"Try to relax," she said. "The more you fight the chills, the worse they get."

His eyes met hers, unexpectedly open. "Stay?"

The single word held none of his usual commanding tone—a simple request that tugged at something deep inside her.

"I'm not going anywhere," she said, surprising herself with how much she meant it.

Hesitantly, she reached out and began to stroke his hair, the dark strands surprisingly silky beneath her fingers. The gesture had a calming effect. His eyes closed, and his breathing evened out. She continued the soothing motion, watching as the tension in his face slowly eased.

"My grandmother used to do this when I was sick," she said softly. "Said it was better medicine than anything from a bottle."

"She was right," he said, voice low. "Smart woman."

"The smartest," she agreed.

She expected him to maintain some distance, to keep that invisible barrier he always seemed to have around him. But as the minutes passed, his posture eased, and he gradually moved closer until his head rested against her thigh.

She froze, uncertain, but he seemed unaware of the intimacy of the position, his fevered body seeking solace.

This was the moment when everything shifted.

She could feel the weight of his head against her leg, the surprising softness of his hair beneath her fingers, the heat radiating from his flushed skin. But it was more than a physical sensation. The man who never showed weakness was now trusting her completely.

This isn't my boss, she thought, the realization striking her with clarity. *This isn't part of the deal. This is just Ronan.* Not Mr. Wilder, not the CEO, not even her fake fiancé. Just the man who played Bach on his cello, who jumped into cold Atlantic water without hesitation, who was now seeking comfort in her presence.

Her heart did a slow turn in her chest as the truth she'd been avoiding crashed over her.

She was in love with him.

She stayed like that, one hand stroking his hair, the other resting on his shoulder, feeling each breath deepen as he finally relaxed into sleep. His shivering subsided, replaced by the even rhythm of deep slumber.

Only when she was certain he was completely asleep, did she dare consider extricating herself.

Moving like someone defusing a bomb, she began the delicate process of freeing herself without waking him.

Finally free, she eased herself off the bed.

He moved and turned his face into the pillow and continued sleeping.

She allowed herself a silent sigh of relief before checking his forehead once more. Still feverish, but the frantic heat had eased. Relief washed through her.

With one last glance she slipped out of the bedroom and headed for the kitchen.

Her grandmother's chicken soup recipe was legendary for its healing properties. Neighbors often requested it during illnesses. The secret was the blend of herbs and slow-simmered bone broth, plus a dash of her grandmother's special ingredient that had only been whispered to her when she turned eighteen.

Now, surveying his kitchen properly for the first time, she discovered what she'd suspected: the refrigerator contained protein shakes, cold brew coffee, and bizarrely, an untouched container of blueberries. The pantry wasn't much better: unopened spice jars, two onions with questionable motives, and carrots that had seen better days. Definitely not the makings of a feast.

She pulled out her phone and placed a grocery delivery order.

After placing it, she realized someone needed to let the office know they wouldn't be in tomorrow. With a sigh, she picked up her phone and called HR.

The voice-mail picked up. She cleared her throat, then did her best impression of someone not unraveling.

"Hi, this is Devney Sinclair. Mr. Wilder has come down with a bug and won't be in tomorrow. I've canceled his meetings and rescheduled the board call. I'll be out as well—I seem to have caught the same thing. Thanks."

She hung up and winced.

The moment the call ended, the truth dawned on her: both of them calling out on a Monday? HR was going to light up like a gossip Christmas tree. She could already hear the whispers:

"They're both out sick today?"

"She's been bringing him coffee every morning…"

"There's definitely something going on."

She dropped her phone onto the counter and groaned.

This wasn't a sick day—it was an RSVP to the rumor mill.

That was a problem for tomorrow, though. Right now, he needed care.

The grocery delivery arrived, and she set to work preparing the soup. The routine was meditative—dicing onions, slicing carrots and celery, searing the chicken before adding the broth. As she worked, the kitchen filled with the comforting aromas of herbs and simmering chicken.

Making this soup—her grandmother's recipe, the one reserved for family. It was the action of a woman who cared deeply, who was pouring her newfound emotions into every carefully measured ingredient.

Her phone rang, and her expression lifted when she saw Lucy's name on the screen. She answered with one hand while stirring the pot with the other.

"Well, well," Lucy said, "if it isn't Mrs. Wilder-to-be. How was the weekend of fake matrimonial bliss?"

"It was…complicated," she said, keeping her voice low. "He jumped into the Atlantic after I fell overboard."

Silence. Then—"I'm sorry, what?"

"I'm fine," she said quickly. "But now he's running a fever of 103, and I'm at his place."

"Oh my God," Lucy said. "You're playing nurse. In his apartment."

"Making my grandmother's chicken soup," she said, adding a pinch of her secret ingredient.

"That's not fake-fiancée behavior. That's real relationship territory, with a side of rom-com."

She froze, wooden spoon midair. "I'm being a decent human being," she said, though the words felt hollow.

"Sure," Lucy said. "Keep telling yourself that. But decent human beings call for help or drop off soup. They don't spend the night and cook family recipes in kitchens that aren't theirs."

Lucy's words echoed her own thoughts with uncomfortable accuracy.

"It's not like that," she said, though the ache in her chest suggested otherwise.

"If you say so," Lucy said, clearly unconvinced. "Be careful, okay? This was supposed to be business, remember?"

"I remember," she said, though the line between business and personal had been obliterated the moment she'd felt his head settle into her lap. "I should go. The soup needs attention."

"The soup needs you," Lucy said. "Right. Call me tomorrow with updates on your patient."

As she hung up and turned back to the simmering pot, Lucy's words echoed in her mind.

Real relationship territory.

She tried to dismiss them, focusing instead on the rhythmic motion of stirring, on the recipe that connected her to her grandmother, on anything but the man sleeping in the next room and the feelings she could no longer ignore.

But the realization had already taken root, and there was no going back.

She was in love with Ronan Wilder. Completely, desperately, hopelessly in love.

And when he recovered—when they returned to their normal roles of boss and assistant—she wasn't sure she'd be able to pretend that nothing had changed.

Chapter 15

HE WOKE to the scent of cooking—rich, savory, and completely foreign in his apartment. For a moment, he couldn't remember where he was or why his body felt like it had been trampled by a herd of investors during a market crash. His limbs felt like dead weight, his throat was raw, and a steady throb in his head signaled a fever still present but no longer raging.

The digital clock on his nightstand blinked 6:17 p.m. in smug fluorescent clarity. He'd slept for hours.

Memories came in fragments—the helicopter ride, the never-ending shivering, her cool palm against his forehead. The weight of her fingers in his hair. The comfort of resting his head in her lap while fever ravaged his defenses.

She'd stayed.

With effort, he pushed himself upright, the room swaying dramatically for a moment. He was still wearing his button-down shirt and slacks, now wrinkled and damp with illness. He peeled off the offending clothes with slow, clumsy fingers and stumbled toward the bathroom, one hand trailing along the wall for balance. The hallway stretched longer than it should have—some fevered trick of perception—but he made it, flicking on the light and flinching at the glare.

The mirror delivered brutal honesty. Dark circles hollowed his eyes, stubble shadowed his jaw, and his skin had the pallor of death warmed over.

The shower helped. Hot water pounded his shoulders. He lingered beneath the spray, letting the steam ease the ache in his joints and clear the mental fog. By the time he emerged, wrapped in a towel he was breathing easier.

He dressed in gray sweatpants and a worn gray T-shirt. He followed the scent of food through the apartment. The closer he got, the more vivid it became—onions, aromatic herbs, the deep richness of slow-simmered broth. He reached the kitchen and stopped short.

The scene before him was one he couldn't have conjured in a fever dream.

She stood with her back to him, stirring a pot on the stove. She'd kicked off her shoes. Her hair was pulled into a messy bun, loose tendrils curling at the nape of her neck. The sleeves of her blouse were rolled to her elbows as she hummed under her breath.

A loaf of crusty bread sat cooling on a rack he didn't recognize. His kitchen looked…lived in. Like someone actually existed here rather than merely occupying space.

She hadn't noticed him yet, so he took another moment to observe this domestic scene. How naturally she inhabited corners of his life he rarely entered himself. How her presence filled spaces he hadn't even realized were empty.

"What is that smell?" he finally said.

She startled, spinning around with a wooden spoon in hand, eyes widening as she took in his appearance.

"Who are you and what have you done with my boss?" she demanded, her gaze traveling from his sweatpants to his T-shirt. "I was convinced you slept in suits."

He leaned against the doorframe, crossing his arms defensively. "I own clothes."

"Clearly," she said, gesturing with the spoon. "Though I have to say, this is not what I pictured. I was expecting monogrammed silk pajamas."

"Sorry to disappoint."

"Not disappointed," she said. "Merely surprised. I have never seen you look so human."

"As opposed to what?"

"CEO robot? Financial terminator?" She gave the pot one last stir before setting the spoon aside. "How are you feeling?"

"Fine."

She gave him a look that combined medical diagnosis with judicial judgment. "So, terrible but maintaining appearances. Got it."

He ignored this assessment, moving further into the kitchen to examine what she was cooking. "What is this?"

"My grandmother's chicken soup," she said. "Guaranteed to cure what ails you, according to everyone who's ever tasted it."

"You made soup," he said. "In my kitchen."

"Well, I didn't make it in the bathroom," she replied. "Though that might have been more sanitary. When was the last time you actually cooked here? Your pots had dust on them."

"The penthouse came fully equipped. I've never had reason to use most of it."

"That's not an answer," she said, ladling soup into a bowl. "Here. Sit. Eat."

"I don't need to be managed," he said, even as he obeyed, settling onto a barstool at his kitchen island.

"Right," she said dryly, setting the steaming bowl before him. "That's why you were shivering with a 103-degree fever earlier. Because you're so excellent at self-care."

He reached for the spoon. "You didn't need to stay."

"Well, someone had to make sure you didn't cook your brain with that fever. Besides," she said, slicing into the bread with her back to him, "I already called us out sick for tomorrow. I'm committed now."

He paused, spoon halfway to his mouth. "You did what?"

"Called us out sick," she said, placing bread beside his bowl. "You have a fever. I've been exposed. It seemed logical."

The soup was extraordinary—rich and complex, with herbs he couldn't identify and a depth that spoke of hours of slow simmering. It was nothing like the bland, mass-produced versions he ordered when working late. This was revelatory.

"Good?" she asked, eyes bright with what looked suspiciously like pride.

He nodded reluctantly. "Acceptable."

"High praise," she said, rolling her eyes as she poured herself a bowl. "Remind me never to cook for you again."

"I didn't ask you to cook for me this time," he pointed out, taking another spoonful. The warmth spread through him, easing aches he hadn't realized he had.

"No, you didn't," she agreed, settling onto the stool beside him. "Consider it a bonus service. I excel at exceeding expectations."

They ate in silence for several minutes, the only sound the gentle clink of spoons against ceramic. It was strange, this comfortable domesticity. Strange and yet not unpleasant. There was an ease to it that felt both foreign and oddly familiar, as if they'd shared countless quiet meals instead of just this one.

His apartment had never felt like this—warm, inhabited, alive.

"You really didn't need to rearrange tomorrow," he said finally, setting his spoon down. "I can manage."

"With what?" she challenged, turning to face him fully.

"You could barely stand upright. And you have the Beauchamp meeting on Wednesday, which you can't afford to miss because you worked yourself into pneumonia."

"It's not pneumonia," he muttered.

"Not yet," she said. "But it will be if you drag yourself into the office tomorrow in some misguided display of corporate martyrdom."

"It's called responsibility."

"It's called stubbornness," she countered. "And it's going to land you in the hospital if you don't take a day to actually recover."

"I don't need a nursemaid," he said stiffly.

"Good, because I'm not offering to be one," she shot back. "I'm being a practical human being who recognizes that sometimes bodies need rest. Even yours, shocking as that may be."

He opened his mouth to argue further but found himself suddenly exhausted. The small burst of energy that had propelled him from bed to kitchen was fading rapidly, leaving him hollow and drained. He pressed his fingers to the bridge of his nose, trying to focus through the returning haze.

"Are we having our first fight?" he asked, surprising himself with the question.

She burst into laughter. "As opposed to what? The daily verbal sparring matches we've engaged in for the past six months?"

Despite himself, he felt the corner of his mouth lift. She had a point. Their professional relationship had always involved a certain amount of intellectual combat. "Fair point."

Her laughter faded, but the warmth in her eyes remained. "Eat your soup. Then you can go back to bed and plot world domination or whatever it is you do when you're not terrorizing boardrooms."

"I don't terrorize boardrooms," he said. "I manage expectations."

"Is that what we're calling it now?" she asked, the teasing note returning to her voice. "I'm sure the intern you made cry last month would disagree."

"He submitted a report with three numerical errors," he said defensively. "In finance, those kinds of mistakes can cost millions."

"And pointing them out privately wouldn't have achieved the same result?"

He considered this, frowning. The question made him uncomfortable because it suggested alternatives he hadn't considered. "It wouldn't have made the same impression."

"On who? The intern or your ego?"

The words stung because they carried truth he didn't want to examine. He'd built his reputation on exacting standards and ruthless efficiency. Fear was a tool, and effective tools weren't discarded. But sitting here in his kitchen, wearing sweatpants and eating homemade soup while she challenged him with gentle persistence, that approach felt suddenly…crude.

"You're bold for someone who commandeered my kitchen," he said, instead of answering directly.

"You're grumpy for someone who got served homemade soup," she countered.

They lapsed into silence again, but it was comfortable rather than tense. The soup was working its magic, lessening illness's grip on his body and clearing his thoughts. He found himself studying her profile as she ate—the way she tucked loose hair behind her ear, the small crease of concentration between her brows.

"It's excellent," he said finally, setting down his empty spoon. "The soup. Thank you."

Something in her expression softened. "You're welcome."

"What's in it? It tastes different from any soup I've had before."

"Family secret," she said. "My grandmother would haunt me if I told you."

"Even your fake fiancé?" he asked, testing the waters with humor while observing her reaction.

Her cheeks flushed, but her voice stayed steady. "Maybe especially my fake fiancé. She'd see right through you, you know. Grandma Sinclair had a sixth sense about people. She'd take one look at those spreadsheets you call a personality and know exactly what we were up to."

"I'm more than spreadsheets," he said, strangely stung by the assessment.

"I know," she said, her voice quieter than expected. "I was joking. You're also quarterly reports and profit margins."

He shook his head, recognizing her attempt to ease the tension. "Hilarious."

"I thought so," she said, standing to clear their bowls. "Now, go back to bed. You still look half-dead, but with slightly more color."

"You don't have to stay," he said again, though the words lacked conviction. The prospect of returning to his empty bedroom, of silence settling back over his apartment like a shroud, created an unexpected hollowness.

She paused, hands full of dishes, and her expression changed. "Do you want me to go?"

The question hung between them, deceptively simple.

"No," he admitted finally. "But you shouldn't feel obligated to stay."

"I don't do obligation," she said, resuming her task of loading dishes into the dishwasher. "Not for things that matter."

The casual way she said it—*things that matter*—sent unexpected warmth through his chest. When had he last mattered to anyone outside of what he could give them or help them to achieve? When had someone stayed simply because they wanted to?

"Thank you," he said finally. "For staying. For the soup. For all of it."

Her expression softened. "You're welcome. Now go rest. The business world will survive."

On the walk back to his bedroom, he couldn't shake the sense that the dynamic between them had shifted into uncharted territory. Not the professional distance they'd maintained, not the careful choreography of their fake engagement, but genuine care freely given.

The thought should have alarmed him. Instead, as he sank back onto his bed, he found himself oddly at peace.

Either way, as sleep claimed him once more, his last conscious thought was of her—the sound of her presence filling his too-quiet world.

<hr>

Chapter 16

<hr>

THE RICH SCENT of coffee nudged her awake, an aroma too real for dreams. She blinked, momentarily disoriented by her surroundings. The sleek leather couch beneath her, the floor-to-ceiling windows showcasing Manhattan's morning skyline.

It took her a moment to remember where she was. His penthouse. The events of yesterday flooded back—his fever, the soup, their surprisingly easy conversation in the kitchen. She must have fallen asleep on his couch after checking on him one last time.

Someone had draped a cashmere throw over her during the night.

The gesture sent unexpected warmth through her. Even while recovering from illness, he'd thought to ensure her comfort. It was such a small kindness, yet it felt monumental given how carefully he guarded his personal space.

"Good morning."

She turned toward the voice, pushing herself upright. He stood in the kitchen doorway, looking remarkably more human than he had yesterday. His color had returned, though shadows still lingered beneath his eyes. He'd exchanged yesterday's sweatpants for dark jeans and a gray Harvard T-shirt that somehow looked expensive despite its simplicity.

"You're up," she said, running a hand through her hopelessly tangled hair.

"Astute observation." His dry tone offered a strange comfort. He gestured behind him. "I ordered breakfast."

She rubbed at her eyes and squinted at him. "You did?"

"From that bakery you mentioned. The one with the strawberry croissants. You once said the powdered sugar they use 'tastes like optimism.'"

She'd made the comment months ago during a particularly stressful morning when he'd been especially demanding and she'd been stress-eating pastries in the break room.

"You remembered that?"

"You talk frequently," he said, tone dry but not unkind. "Some of it registers."

The casual way he dismissed his own thoughtfulness made her chest ache. This man who claimed to hate distractions had remembered her ridiculous metaphor from three months ago and acted on it.

"Thank you," she said quietly.

He nodded once, uncomfortable with her gratitude. "Don't expect it to become routine."

But she was already beginning to hope it might.

She untangled herself from the throw and walked toward the kitchen, conscious of her rumpled clothes and the fact that she probably looked like she'd been sleeping on couches. The kitchen counter held an assortment of fruit, yogurt parfaits, and pastries, including her favorite strawberry croissants.

"Impressive," she said, reaching for the coffeepot. "Especially for someone who was delirious with fever yesterday."

"I wasn't delirious," he objected, leaning against the counter.

"You curled up in my lap like a cat."

A flush crept up her neck at the memory of his head against her thigh, his arm slung across her legs. The weight of him, so solid and trusting in her arms.

"A momentary lapse in judgment."

"A sweet momentary lapse," she corrected, pouring herself coffee. "But don't worry, your secret's safe with me. I won't tell anyone you enjoy being comforted when you're sick."

"I do not enjoy—" He stopped, shaking his head. "You're baiting me."

"Always," she said cheerfully, taking a sip of coffee. It was perfect—strong but not bitter, exactly how she liked it. "You even got my coffee right."

"You've mentioned your preferences often enough," he said, but the words lacked their usual edge.

She selected a strawberry croissant from the bakery box and settled onto one of the bar stools, studying him. "You're looking better, but you should still take it easy."

"I'm well enough to go to the office," he said, already sounding decided. "I have meetings I need to—"

"Nope," she interrupted, popping the 'p' with too much enthusiasm. "We already called out sick. The meetings are rescheduled. You are officially on sick leave today."

"Devney—"

"Ronan," she countered, mimicking his authoritative tone perfectly. "You worked all weekend at the Beauchamps'. You need to rest."

He gave her an incredulous look. "Sailing and dinner parties are hardly work."

"Aren't they, though?" she challenged, setting down her coffee. "Think about it. We couldn't let our guard down for a single minute. Every conversation, every gesture, every look was part of a performance. That's more exhausting than any board meeting."

He paused, considering her words. "You seemed to excel at it."

"I was terrified the entire time," she admitted. "One wrong word and the whole charade falls apart. That's work. Emotional work."

"I hadn't considered it as stressful as work," he said, his voice quieter.

"Most people don't," she said. "But trust me, playing a role, even one you're good at, is draining. Add in a dip in the Atlantic, fever, and our usual workload, and it's a recipe for getting sick all over again." She took another sip of coffee, holding his gaze. "So. One day. To recover. Is that really so unreasonable?"

He frowned, but she could tell she was winning. "What exactly would this 'recovery day' entail?"

"Normal human activities," she said. "Food. Rest. Maybe a movie or two."

"Movies," he repeated, as if she'd suggested competitive yodeling.

"Yes, movies. Those things with pictures and sounds that tell stories." She tilted her head, studying him. "Don't tell me you don't watch movies."

"I watch documentaries," he said defensively.

"Of course you do," she laughed. "Let me guess—financial histories and exposés of corporate scandals?"

"There's nothing wrong with being informed about one's industry."

"Nothing at all. But today is about recovery, which means actual relaxation. Entertainment."

"I'm not watching romantic comedies," he said, his expression so genuinely alarmed that she had to bite back laughter.

"What do you have against romantic comedies? Afraid you might crack an expression? Or worse, have an emotion?"

He rolled his eyes, but she caught the slight lift of his lips.

"I prefer entertainment with some basis in reality."

"Says the guy who reads financial projections for fun," she teased. "Fine, no rom-coms. We'll find middle ground."

She glanced down at her wrinkled clothes. "But first, I need to freshen up. Any chance you have clothes I could borrow? I'd rather not spend the day in yesterday's outfit."

He looked momentarily taken aback, as if the request puzzled him.

"I…suppose I could find an option."

"Nothing fancy," she assured him. "A T-shirt would be fine. The stuff I packed for the weekend is still in your car, and I'm not exactly up for a wardrobe run right now."

He nodded, setting down his coffee. "I'll see what I can do."

While he disappeared into his bedroom, she helped herself to another pastry and explored the living room more thoroughly than she'd had time for yesterday. Like everything else in his home, it was elegant, expensive, and oddly impersonal. No family photos, no mementos, nothing that revealed the man behind the wealth.

The only hint of personality was the bookshelf tucked into the corner. Filled with well-read paperbacks showing clear signs of use—creased spines, bent corners, curling pages softened by handling. She ran her fingers along the titles, discovering an eclectic mix of classics and contemporary fiction. Hemingway next to Murakami. Austen beside McEwan.

"Here," his voice startled her. He stood a few feet away, holding out a neatly folded Harvard T-shirt and what looked like drawstring pajama pants. "These should work."

She glanced at the identical logo on the shirt he was wearing.

"Wait, will we both be wearing Harvard?" she asked.

He looked down, then back at her. "Completely unintentional."

She laughed. "Adorable. Do we get monogrammed robes next? Maybe matching crests?"

"You're welcome," he grumbled, but there was no heat in it.

She headed to the bathroom, marveling again at the marble-and-glass luxury. She washed her face, grateful for the unopened toothbrush and toothpaste he'd thoughtfully included with the clothes.

His T-shirt was unsurprisingly soft, probably some ridiculously expensive cotton despite its simple appearance. It hung loose on her frame, reaching mid-thigh. The crimson Harvard logo had faded from many washings, making it somehow more intimate than if it had been new. She had to cinch the drawstring pants tight and roll the waistband to keep them from falling down.

When she emerged, he was on the couch, scrolling through his tablet. He looked up, and something quick and unreadable flickered in his eyes before his expression became neutral again.

"Better?" he asked, his voice oddly tight.

"Much," she said, moving across the room to join him. "Thanks for the clothes. Very Ivy League chic."

He cleared his throat, setting the tablet aside. "I was reviewing the streaming options. Since you've insisted on this… relaxation day."

"Look at you, already embracing the plan," she said, curling up at the opposite end of the couch. "What did you find?"

"Nothing with singing, dancing, or improbable romantic scenarios," he said firmly.

"Killjoy cinema it is," she said with a grin. "Let me see."

They eventually settled on a thriller that promised enough intelligence to satisfy him and enough actual plot to keep her entertained. As the movie began, she was acutely conscious of the deliberate space between them—necessary but somehow ridiculous.

The cognitive dissonance was striking. They'd maintained a careful professional distance for months, yet here she sat in his living room, wearing his Harvard T-shirt, about to spend the day watching movies. The intimacy of it should have felt strange, but instead it felt right.

About twenty minutes in, she pulled the cashmere throw over her legs, suppressing a shiver. The air conditioning in his penthouse was set to arctic levels.

"Cold?" he asked, noticing the movement.

"A little," she admitted. "Do you keep it this cool for the penguins you're secretly harboring?"

"I can adjust the thermostat."

"No need," she said, tucking the throw more securely around her. "I'm fine."

He studied her for a moment before returning his attention to the screen. Ten minutes later, she felt the cushions shift as he moved closer.

"They're about to reveal the entire premise is flawed," he said, nodding toward the screen. "The security system they're trying to breach can't actually be bypassed that way."

She turned to look at him. "Are you secretly a hacker in your spare time?"

"No, but I sit on the board of a cybersecurity firm. The technical consultant for this film clearly took creative liberties."

"It's Hollywood," she said. "Creative liberties are the whole point."

"It wouldn't have been difficult to make it accurate," he insisted. "Here, look—" He leaned closer, gesturing toward the screen as he explained details about authentication protocols that she only half-followed.

What caught her attention instead was the animated way

he spoke when discussing a topic he knew well. And his proximity.

Her pulse quickened at his nearness. She could smell his soap, feel the warmth radiating from his body. The casual intimacy of the moment—him in a T-shirt and jeans, explaining movie plot holes while sitting close enough that their knees almost touched.

"You're not listening," he said.

"I'm listening. Authentication protocols. Fascinating."

He gave her a look that said he wasn't fooled. "My point is the film loses credibility when they get these details wrong."

"But most people don't watch thrillers for their technical accuracy. They watch for the story, the tension, the characters."

"The mistakes distract from those elements."

"Only if you know they're wrong. Which most people don't. It's like me watching a movie about art forgery—I'd probably miss all kinds of details that would drive an actual art expert crazy."

He considered this, then nodded slowly. "Fair point."

She grinned, delighted by this small victory. "Did you admit I was right about a topic? Alert the media."

"Don't let it go to your head."

As the movie continued, the careful distance between them continued to diminish and by the climactic scene, their shoulders were touching, and she was hyperaware of every point of contact. The brush of his arm against hers when he reached for his water glass. The way he leaned closer when making another commentary about the film's technical flaws. The steady rhythm of his breathing, which she found oddly soothing.

When he suggested a second movie, she agreed, and during the opening credits, she found herself tucked against his side, his arm draped casually around her shoulders.

This was dangerous territory, she knew. The line between

their professional relationship and personal feelings was blurring. But sitting there in his arms, sharing this quiet morning, she found it impossible to care about the consequences.

When the credits rolled on the second film, neither of them moved to reach for the remote. The silence stretched between them, heavy with unspoken tension.

"That was…" he said, his voice quieter than usual.

"Completely implausible?" she suggested, turning to face him.

"I was going to say entertaining," he said. "Despite the technical flaws."

The cashmere throw had slipped during the movie, and she pulled it back up.

His gaze lingered on the borrowed T-shirt before meeting her eyes. The air between them shifted, charged with electricity that had nothing to do with fever or gratitude or pretense.

"Devney," he said, her name coming out rougher than usual.

"Yes?" The word was barely a whisper.

He reached over, his fingers brushing her cheek with surprising gentleness. This touch was different from any before —intentional, loaded with meaning she didn't dare interpret. "Thank you. For staying. For taking care of me."

"You already thanked me," she said, but she didn't pull away from his touch.

His thumb traced along her jawline, and she felt her breath catch. "I don't know how to do this."

"Do what?"

"This," he said, his voice dropping lower. "Whatever this is between us."

The space between them seemed to shrink without either of them moving. She could see the flecks of gold in his dark eyes, could feel the warmth radiating from his body despite the fact that his fever had broken hours ago.

"Ronan," she breathed.

"Tell me to stop," he said, echoing words from some half-remembered dream. "Tell me this is just me being grateful, or the fever talking, or—"

She silenced him by closing the distance between them, her lips meeting his in a kiss that was soft at first, tentative. Testing. But when he responded, his hand sliding into her hair to cradle the back of her head, the kiss deepened.

This was what had been building between them all morning—all weekend.

When they broke apart, both breathing unsteadily, she searched his face for any sign of regret or uncertainty.

Instead, she found heat.

"Is this just you being grateful?" she asked quietly.

"No," he said firmly, his voice rough with certainty. "It's not."

"And it's not the fever."

"Definitely not the fever." His thumb brushed across her bottom lip, still damp from their kiss. "Though I might be delirious for entirely different reasons."

She laughed softly, and the sound seemed to undo his restraint completely. His other arm came around her waist, pulling her closer until she was practically in his lap.

"Are you sure?" he asked against her mouth. "Because once we cross this line…"

"I'm sure," she whispered, and then she was kissing him again, deeper this time, with a hunger that seemed to match the intensity of his response.

His hands found the hem of the Harvard T-shirt, and she lifted her arms as he pulled it over her head. She heard his sharp intake of breath when he realized she wasn't wearing anything underneath.

"Beautiful," he murmured, his voice reverent as his hands

mapped the curves of her body with deliberate slowness. "So beautiful."

She tugged at his shirt in response, and he helped her remove it, revealing the lean muscle she'd only glimpsed in his fevered moments. Her hands explored the planes of his chest, tracing the defined lines of his torso, feeling his heart racing under her palms.

When he lifted her fully into his lap, she could feel his arousal pressing against her through the thin cotton of their clothes. The friction made her gasp, and he captured the sound with his mouth, his tongue teasing hers as his hands slipped beneath the waistband of the borrowed pants to grip her bare skin.

"Your bedroom," she managed between kisses.

"Too far," he said roughly, his hands sliding down to cup her through the cotton, making her arch against him.

"Ronan," she protested, even as she moved against him, creating more of that delicious friction.

"Here," he said, his mouth moving to her neck, finding that spot that made her arch against him. "Right here, where you made me feel human again."

His words undid her completely. She fumbled with the button of his jeans, and he lifted his hips to help her push them down along with his boxers. When she rose up on her knees to shimmy out of the borrowed pants, his hands guided her movements, his eyes dark with want as he took in every inch of revealed skin.

The rest of their clothes disappeared with urgency, and then there was nothing between them but skin and desire and the desperate need to be closer.

He took his time exploring her body with reverent touches, his mouth following the path of his hands until she was trembling with need. His lips traced a path down her throat to her collarbone, then lower, lavishing attention on her breasts until she was gasping his name. When his hand slipped between her legs, finding her slick and ready, she cried out at the intimate contact.

"Please," she whispered, her voice breaking on the word.

He positioned her above him, his hands gripping her hips as she braced herself on his shoulders. They both went still for a moment, the magnitude of what they were about to do settling between them.

"Are you sure?" he asked one more time, his voice strained with the effort of holding back.

Instead of answering with words, she kissed him as she slowly lowered herself onto him, taking him inch by deliberate inch. The sensation was overwhelming—he filled her completely, stretching her in the most perfect way, as if they'd been made for each other.

"God," he groaned against her mouth, his control fraying as she began to move. "You feel incredible."

She set a slow rhythm at first, savoring the way he felt inside her, the way his hands guided her movements. But as the tension built between them, their pace became more urgent, more desperate.

He pulled her close, changing the angle so that every move-ment sent sparks through her core. When she was close to the edge, he would slow their rhythm, keeping her balanced on the precipice until she was trembling and pleading.

"Not yet," he murmured against her ear, his voice dark with control and promise. "I want to feel you fall apart in my arms."

The combination of his words and the exquisite torture of being held at the brink made her wild with need. When he finally allowed her to chase her release, the climax crashed over her with devastating intensity, her body clenching around him as she cried out his name.

The sight and feel of her coming undone triggered his

own. He buried his face in her neck as he emptied himself inside her, his body shuddering with the force of it.

Afterward, they stayed tangled together on the couch, her head on his shoulder, both of them breathing hard.

"Well," she said eventually, her voice hoarse. "That was worth the sick day."

"Best recovery plan I've ever had," he agreed, his voice rough with satisfaction.

She lifted her head to look at him, her expression growing serious. "You really did scare me yesterday."

His expression shifted. "I'm not used to having someone worry about me."

"Get used to it," she said, then blushed as she realized how that sounded. "I mean, if you want…if this isn't just…"

He silenced her with a kiss, soft and sure. "This isn't just anything," he said when they broke apart. "This is everything."

The words hung between them, heavy with implication and promise. Neither of them was ready to examine what "everything" meant, but for now, it was enough.

As the sun set over Manhattan, casting golden light through the floor-to-ceiling windows, they made love again—slower this time, with the luxury of exploration and the knowledge that they had all night. He worshipped her body with his hands and mouth until she was boneless with pleasure, then loved her with a tenderness that brought tears to her eyes.

And when she finally fell asleep in his bed, her head on his chest and her hand over his heart, the steady rhythm beneath her palm carried her into dreams where the line between pretense and reality had disappeared completely.

Chapter 17

HE WOKE BEFORE HIS ALARM, which rarely happened anymore. Silk sheets and the quiet hum of the city below greeted him as consciousness returned. For a moment, he lay still, surprised by the contentment that had settled deep within him. Then he became aware of the warm weight pressed against his side.

Devney was curled next to him, one hand splayed across his chest, her hair cascading across his pillow. She was wearing his Harvard T-shirt again, and nothing else, and the sight of her bare legs tangled with his sent heat straight to his core.

Memories of the night before crashed over him, her hands on his skin, the taste of her mouth, the way she'd whispered his name in the darkness. They'd made love twice more after that first desperate coupling on the couch, each time slower and more thorough than the last.

She stirred against him, her palm pressing more firmly against his ribs, and he felt her body come awake.

"Good morning," he said, his voice rough with sleep.

"Mmm." She lifted her head to look at him, and he was

struck by how natural she looked in his bed, how right this felt. "How did you sleep?"

"Better than I have in months," he admitted, then caught her hand and pressed it to his lips. "And you?"

She smiled, her fingers tracing along his jaw. "Like I belonged here."

"You do," he said without thinking, then paused as the weight of those words settled between them.

Her eyes softened. "Do I?"

"More than you know," he said, rolling her beneath him and capturing her mouth in a kiss that tasted like forever.

He'd showered first, and when Devney disappeared into the bathroom, he asked the doorman to bring her clothes up from the car. By the time they made it to the kitchen an hour later, she was in the pretty blue summer dress they'd picked out for the weekend in Martha's Vineyard. The dynamic between them had shifted into new territory. Not the deliberate distance they'd maintained before, but not quite the easy intimacy they'd shared in his sickness either.

This was uncharted territory for both of them.

The morning routine felt different now—charged with new awareness. He set out the pastries and fruit from the bakery delivery while she perched on a barstool, watching him with curious eyes.

"Coffee?" he offered, reaching for the expensive machine that dominated one corner of his kitchen.

"Please." She smoothed her dress with nervous energy. "So. We should talk about…yesterday. Last night."

He paused in his coffee preparation, understanding her need to define what had happened between them. "What about it?"

"What it means. For us. For work. For this whole fake engagement thing."

He set her coffee in front of her. "What do you want it to mean?"

"That's not an answer," she said, taking a sip and sighing with pleasure.

"It's the only answer I have right now," he admitted. "I don't have a protocol for this situation."

"The great Ronan Wilder, stumped by a simple relationship question." There was an edge of vulnerability in her voice.

"There's nothing simple about this," he said. "About you. About what I feel when I'm with you."

Her eyes softened. "What do you feel?"

He was quiet for a moment, struggling to put into words emotions he'd never experienced before. "Like I've been sleep-walking through my life, and you woke me up."

The admission hung between them, more revealing than any physical intimacy they'd shared.

"Ronan," she said.

"I know it makes things complex," he continued. "The business arrangement, our working relationship, everything. But I can't pretend last night didn't happen. I can't pretend I don't want it to happen again."

"I don't want to pretend either," she said. "But we need to be smart about this. At work, we still need to maintain some level of boundaries."

"Agreed." Though even as he said it, he was imagining how difficult it would be to maintain workplace distance when all he wanted was to pull her back into his arms.

"And the fake engagement…do we keep that going? With the Beauchamps, I mean."

It was a practical question, but it struck him with unexpected force. Because somewhere in the space between fevered dreams and the morning light, the engagement had stopped feeling fake to him.

"We'll figure it out," he said. "Together."

She nodded, seeming satisfied with that answer. "Together."

The word felt like a promise.

They rode to work in his car, maintaining deliberate space between them but stealing glances when they thought the other wasn't looking. The sexual tension was palpable, a live wire connecting them across the leather seats.

When they arrived at Oath Capital, he spotted the florist in the lobby and made a quick decision.

"Go ahead up," he said, nodding toward the elevators. "I need to have a quick word with security about a matter. I'll be right behind you."

She nodded. "Good thinking. We shouldn't arrive together anyway, people will wonder."

The moment the elevator doors closed behind her, he turned and strode toward the flower shop. The impulse took over—he had to get her flowers. Not just any flowers.

"Sunflowers," he said to the florist before she could even greet him properly. "The brightest ones you have."

The woman smiled as she selected a vibrant bunch. "Someone special?"

"Very," he said without hesitation, surprising himself with how easily the admission came.

The elevator ride up gave him time to second-guess the purchase, but when the doors opened and he saw her at her desk, arranging files with that focused expression he'd come to love, he knew he'd made the right choice.

Sunflowers. Bright and bold and her favorite.

He walked to her desk, aware that half the office was watching.

"Thank you," he said, his voice low as he set the sunflowers down. "For everything."

Her eyes widened, then her cheeks flushed pink. "You didn't have to—"

"I wanted to," he said.

Their fingers brushed when she reached for the flowers, and the small contact sent electricity straight through him.

This was going to be impossible.

"Mr. Wilder," she said, her voice composed and businesslike. "You have the Beauchamp call at ten, and the quarterly review meeting at two."

"Of course," he said. "And Devney?"

"Yes, sir?"

The formality was killing him. "Excellent work yesterday. Taking care of things."

The double meaning wasn't lost on either of them. He had to force himself to turn away before he did anything unprofessional like kiss her in front of the entire office.

As he headed to his office, he heard Knox's laughter echoing down the hallway.

Yes, this was going to be a problem.

But as he settled behind his desk and caught sight of Devney arranging the sunflowers in a vase, her face soft with pleasure, he found he didn't care about problems or obstacles or the structured routine he'd built his life around.

Some things were worth the chaos.

And she was worth everything.

The morning slipped by in a flurry of emails, meetings, and phone calls. But no matter how focused he tried to be, his eyes kept drifting through the glass wall of his office to her desk, where she sat working with the sunflowers brightening her workspace.

Every interaction felt charged. When she brought him coffee, her fingers lingered against his as she passed him the cup. When she leaned over his desk to point out a detail in a report, he caught the scent of her perfume and remembered how it had clung to his sheets that morning.

By lunchtime, he was losing his mind.

Knox appeared in his doorway, arms crossed and wearing a knowing smirk. "So. Interesting development with you and Devney."

"I don't know what you mean," he said, not looking up from his computer screen.

"Right." Knox stepped into the office, closing the door behind him. "Half the office is convinced you two are sleeping together."

His head snapped up. "What?"

"Relax. It's speculation based on the way you can't stop looking at her, and the way she blushes every time you walk by her desk." Knox settled into the chair across from him. "Plus, there was that little moment this morning where you laughed. In public. People are starting to think you've been replaced by a human."

"Knox—"

"I'm not judging," Knox said, holding up his hands. "I'm impressed. I didn't think you had it in you to break the pact for anyone, but she's special."

The pact. The agreement they'd made in college about staying single until forty. A promise that felt like a lifetime ago.

"It's complex," he said.

"The best things usually are." The expression on Knox's face grew more serious. "But you know this could get messy, right? Office relationships, power dynamics, all that HR nightmare stuff?"

"I'm aware of the challenges."

"Are you? Because from where I'm sitting, it looks like you're falling hard and fast, and you've never had to navigate anything like this before." Knox paused. "What happens when the fake engagement story falls apart? When Beauchamp finds out you've been lying to him?"

"We'll figure it out," he said.

"You'd better," Knox stood. "Because if this goes sideways, it won't just be your heart on the line. They will be affected, too."

After Knox left, he sat staring at his computer screen. The rational part of his mind knew he was right. This was dangerous territory, both for him and for business.

But then he caught sight of Devney through the glass, laughing at something a coworker said. She was radiant, alive in a way that made his chest constrict with want and feeling.

He was falling, had already fallen, and for the first time in his methodical life he didn't have a plan for what came next.

Chapter 18

SHE WAS in her own apartment, surrounded by the usual chaos of her real life—wilting plants, an overflowing laundry basket, a refrigerator holding nothing but expired yogurt and takeout containers—while her mind stayed trapped somewhere else entirely, replaying every moment in his penthouse, every touch, every whispered word. She had been swept away by a night of incredible sex with her boss.

The question was, what happened now?

By the time she showered, dressed, and flagged down a cab on the corner, nothing felt settled. The city slid past the windows in a blur while her body still carried him, while her thoughts kept drifting back to the way he had looked at her, the way he had held her.

At work, the sunflowers from yesterday waited in their crystal vase. Her favorite flowers, something she had mentioned once in passing, and he had remembered.

When the elevator chimed fifteen minutes later, she looked up to see him walking toward her in a charcoal suit that made her mouth go dry. Their eyes met across the office, and the professional greeting she had rehearsed never made it past her lips.

He looked at her like she was everything he'd been thinking about. Whatever this was between them, they were both in far deeper than either of them had anticipated.

She settled into her chair, but her focus was a lost cause, her gaze constantly snagging on the man behind the glass. Ronan sat with his head bent over reports, the distance between them feeling like a canyon instead of a few feet of office space. He looked up once, trapping her stare. A sharp, unfamiliar tightness lived in the corners of his eyes before he abruptly dropped his attention back to the page.

Was that regret? The warmth of the morning felt suddenly fragile, like a temporary glitch in the cold, efficient machinery of his life. Maybe she had simply been a convenient comfort during a fever, a variable he was already calculating how to move to the "resolved" column.

Her phone buzzed.

LUCY: Lunch today? Need gossip that isn't about flour ratios.

She typed back a quick confirmation.

By noon, the tension around her had wound so tight inside her that she couldn't take another minute. She grabbed her purse and practically fled the office.

Outside, she hailed a cab. As Manhattan blocks rolled past the window, she hoped the distance would help clear her head. But every mile between them felt like a mistake.

The cab pulled up outside Lucy's bakery, and she paid the driver. Through the window, she could see Lucy finishing up with a customer. When Lucy spotted her through the glass, she held up one finger, mouthed "just a minute."

A few moments later, Lucy emerged from the bakery.

"Thank God you're here," Lucy said. "I was about to lose my mind if I had to discuss fondant techniques one more time today."

"That bad?"

"My last customer wanted to debate the merits of buttercream versus cream cheese frosting for twenty minutes," Lucy said, then paused as they reached the café entrance, studying Devney's face. "But judging by your expression, I'm guessing frosting is the least of our problems today."

They found their usual booth in the back corner, away from the lunch crowd. Lucy waited until they'd ordered. "Spill."

"Ronan bought me flowers yesterday."

"Wait, Mr. Spreadsheet himself? Voluntarily purchased flowers?"

"Sunflowers. He remembered what I told him about my grandmother." She traced the rim of her water glass. "And two nights ago. She looked up, heart pounding. "We made love."

Lucy sat up straighter. "I knew this was real."

"It's complicated. The office is already starting to talk because we were both out sick the same day."

"But there was a real moment between you, right?" Lucy pressed, her eyes bright. "Not a fake-fiancée moment."

"Yes. Many moments."

"And how do you feel about that?" Lucy asked.

The question cut straight to her core.

"I'm in love with him," she said, the words barely audible.

"Finally," Lucy breathed, reaching across the table to squeeze her hand. "Took you long enough to admit it."

"You were right. That day in the bakery. You saw it before I did."

"I've been seeing it for months. Way before this whole fake engagement thing. The way you talk about him, the way your face lights up even when you're complaining about his impossible standards."

She covered her face with her hands. "This is bad, Lucy. So bad."

"Why? Because you're feeling real things for your fake fiancé?" Lucy took Devney's hands from her face, forcing her to look up. "That seems reasonable to me."

"He's my boss," she said. "Julia from Accounting cornered me in the break room this morning asking if I was 'feeling better,' looking like she'd already written the headline."

Lucy winced. "Subtle."

"Not remotely. And now I'm expected to act like it's business as usual, while juggling all these real feelings."

"The fake engagement was his idea, remember? And now he's buying you flowers and making love to you. That doesn't exactly scream emotional detachment."

A wish stirred to life inside her. "You think so?"

"Men rarely buy flowers for women they're indifferent to, especially men like him, who probably consider floral arrangements a wasteful allocation of resources."

Despite herself, she laughed. "That does sound like him."

"Look." Lucy's expression turned serious. "I'm not saying this is simple. The whole boss-employee thing is bound to get messy. But denying how you feel won't make it any clearer."

"So, what do I do?"

Lucy shrugged. "Be honest with yourself, at least. And maybe, when this Beauchamp deal is over, be honest with him, too."

The thought gripped her with terror. "What if I'm reading emotions into an encounter that was just good sex?"

Lucy studied her face. "Is that what you really think happened?"

"I don't know," she admitted, her voice small. "The sunflowers, the way he looked at me in the moment, it felt like there was deeper meaning to it all. But maybe I'm seeing what I want to see because I'm in love with him."

"Or maybe you're so scared of being vulnerable that you're looking for reasons to doubt what could be real," Lucy said gently. "That's more your style."

"Style is one word for it," she said, staring down at her barely touched lunch.

"Promise me something," Lucy said, waiting until she looked up. "Don't make any rash decisions. Don't run away if things get scary. You tend to bail when emotions get too real."

She wanted to argue but couldn't. Lucy knew her too well. "I promise to try."

"Good enough for now."

The rest of lunch passed with Lucy steering the conversation to safer topics.

After lunch, she was hyperaware of every glance, every movement from his office. She caught him watching her through the glass more than once. Each time their eyes met, electricity sparked between them—a connection that felt both new and inevitable.

She checked her watch: two-thirty. Only thirty minutes until Andrew Beauchamp and his team would arrive. This investment deal was crucial for him.

He emerged from his office, stopping at her desk with a folder in hand. "Here is the final presentation for Beauchamp. "Can you check that the conference room is prepared? Make sure the refreshments are set up?"

"Already done," she said, accepting the folder. Their fingers brushed, lingering a fraction longer than necessary. "The room is ready. Everything is set."

"Perfect," he said. "Everything needs to go well."

He hesitated, as if there was more he wanted to say. "Devney," he began, voice dropping lower.

Her heart stuttered. "Yes?"

The elevator chimed. Julia from Accounting stepped into view, eyes narrowing with interest.

"Let me know when they arrive," he said, turning back toward his office.

"Of course." She ignored the disappointment she felt.

Julia approached her desk, a folder clutched in her arms, questions plain on her face. "You two seem close."

She kept her expression impassive. "I'm his assistant. It's part of the job."

"Right. The job that kept you both out sick on Monday?"

"I caught whatever he had. Occupational hazard."

"Must be, considering how much time you two spend together." Julia's gaze sharpened, her tone shifting with it, cool and composed, like she'd been waiting for the perfect moment to say it. "People are talking, you know."

She gave the woman a cool look. "Did you need something, Julia?"

"Dropping off the expense reports," she said, placing the folder on Devney's desk. She leaned closer, voice lowering. "For what it's worth, I think you two make a lovely couple. Though usually office romances don't involve the CEO."

"It's not what you think," Devney said, heart racing.

"The sunflowers suggest otherwise," Julia said, glancing meaningfully at the bright blooms. "Not to mention the way he looks at you when he thinks no one's watching."

With that parting shot, Julia sashayed back toward her desk, leaving Devney staring after her.

What exactly were they? Were they dating? Having a fling?

She realized she had no idea what to call what was happening between them. And that terrified her almost as much as her feelings for him.

At five minutes to three, the elevator doors opened. Andrew Beauchamp stepped out, flanked by his assistant and two associates.

She rose from her desk and moved to greet them. "Mr. Beauchamp, welcome," she said, extending her hand. "I'll let Ronan know you've arrived."

Ronan appeared at her side. "Andrew," he greeted, extending his hand. "Right on time."

"Good to see you again, Wilder," Andrew said, clasping his hand firmly. "Shall we get started?"

"Of course." Ronan placed his hand on the small of her back. "Let's head to the conference room. Everything is ready."

As they walked down the hall, he led the way with her beside him, his hand remaining at her back while Andrew and his team followed. When they reached the conference room, his hand dropped as he prepared to open the door. Before doing so, he leaned close to her, his breath against her ear.

"Ready?" he murmured, voice low enough that only she could hear.

She turned to face him, their faces mere inches apart. "Yes."

His gaze dropped to her lips, and then with a subtle gesture hidden from the Beauchamp party, he reached for her hand, giving it a quick squeeze before releasing it to open the door.

The meeting stretched for two hours, with him masterfully presenting his expansion plans and fielding questions. Throughout it all, she felt his gaze returning to her again and again, as if drawing strength from her presence. When Andrew finally nodded his approval and slid the signed investment papers across the table, Ronan's eyes found hers immediately, bright with triumph.

"I look forward to seeing where you take this," Andrew said, rising to shake his hand.

"We appreciate your confidence in us," he replied.

As they escorted the Beauchamp party to the elevator, the

reality settled over her. The charade had served its purpose. Andrew had signed the investment deal.

Back in the office, a champagne toast with the team celebrated the successful deal. The atmosphere was electric. This investment meant expansion, security, growth. As glasses clinked and congratulations flowed, she stood slightly apart, watching him accept handshakes and backslaps from the department heads.

She caught fragments of whispered conversations as she moved through the gathering—*sleeping with the boss … you don't bring someone flowers like that unless…figured trouble was going on between those two…*

The words stung. What they'd shared had been real and was now reduced to office gossip and speculation.

She noticed Julia from Accounting huddled with two other women from Finance, their eyes shifting toward her. Everything she'd worked for, every boundary she'd tried to maintain crumbled under their scrutiny.

But more than that, she needed to protect what she and Ronan had found together. Whatever it was—love, attraction, something precious and fragile—it didn't deserve to be torn apart by office vultures.

She moved to the center of the room and cleared her throat. Several heads turned in her direction.

"Excuse me," she said, her voice carrying across the space. More conversations halted, attention shifting toward her. "I'd like to say something."

The room hushed. Across the gathering, she could see Ronan looking up. When their eyes met, his expression shifted to alarm.

"I know there have been rumors circulating," she said, her heart hammering against her ribs. "About Mr. Wilder and me."

The silence in the room deepened. Across the room,

Ronan's face had gone pale, and he was subtly shaking his head at her, a desperate warning in his eyes.

"I want to be clear about one detail. We are not dating. We are not anything but boss and assistant." The lie burned as it left her mouth.

"We created this fiction to present a united front for the Beauchamp deal," she explained, her voice strong. "It was a business strategy, nothing more. And it worked. The deal you're celebrating right now? It secured all of your jobs for the long term. So instead of gossiping about my personal life, perhaps you could focus on that."

She could see the horror on Ronan's face, but she felt only the rush of defiant satisfaction. Let them judge her for being strategic.

"The relationship, all of it, was carefully orchestrated to give Mr. Wilder the family-man image that Beauchamp values," she continued, each word a betrayal of her own heart. "We played our roles, we got the contract, and now it's done."

The room was dead silent. Shocked expressions surrounded her.

Then she noticed everyone's eyes had shifted to a spot behind her.

She turned, and the blood drained from her face. Andrew Beauchamp stood in the doorway, his expression unreadable.

"I believe I left my phone in the conference room," Andrew said, his voice cutting through the stunned silence.

The full magnitude of what she'd done crashed over her.

The silence stretched, unbearable and absolute.

"Mr. Beauchamp," she started, her voice barely audible. "I can explain—"

Andrew held up a hand, stopping her words. "I think you've explained quite enough, Ms. Sinclair." He turned toward Ronan. "It seems we have matters to discuss." Andrew turned and walked back toward the conference room, Ronan's eyes met hers one last time across the shocked gathering. The betrayal and devastation she saw there would haunt her forever.

Without a word, he followed Andrew, leaving her standing alone in the center of the silent room.

Chapter 19

THE SILENCE that followed him into the conference room. The sound of everything he'd built beginning to crumble.

He kept his spine straight, his expression impassive, a careful shield over the rage and disbelief churning inside him. Not at her. At himself. At the catastrophic series of miscalculations that had brought them to this moment.

Andrew stood at the window, facing the Manhattan skyline, silhouetted against the glass. When the door clicked shut behind them, he didn't turn.

"How much of it was a lie?" he asked, his voice calm.

He had navigated hostile takeovers, weathered market crashes, stared down boardrooms of adversaries. None of it had prepared him for this—the disappointment of a man he respected.

"The engagement," he answered. "Only the engagement."

Andrew turned, his expression hidden by the late afternoon shadows. "Only?" He gave a humorless laugh. "You built an elaborate scheme to manipulate me into signing a multi-million-dollar investment deal, and you qualify it with 'only?'" Each word landed with precision.

Andrew approached the conference table, his fingers tracing the folder containing the contract they'd signed an hour earlier. "Do you know why I chose Oath Capital? Out of all the investment opportunities that cross my desk every day?"

"Our growth projections. Our track record," he answered, the response automatic, even as it rang false to him.

"No. Those made you a candidate. What sealed my decision was you."

He hadn't expected that. He waited, the control he prided himself on beginning to slip.

"I have watched your career for years," Andrew continued. "Brilliant. Ruthless. Effective. But alone. A lone wolf building an empire." His eyes met Ronan's, sharp with disappointment. "Then you had a partner. Someone who softened your edges. I saw it at the gala—or thought I did. The way you two complemented each other."

He tapped the contract with one finger. "It reminded me of Eleanor and myself. And I thought—he understands what sustains success. Not numbers, but connection. Partnership. More than yourself to work for."

Andrew's words stirred thoughts he'd kept hidden from himself these past weeks.

"I believed in the man I saw when you were with her," Andrew continued, voice hard. "I invested in that man. But he doesn't exist. He was nothing but another fabricated strategy."

Ronan struggled for words. "It's more complex than that."

"Is it?" Andrew asked. "Enlighten me."

How could he explain what he scarcely understood himself? The way the lines had blurred. That strange ache he'd felt when she'd stood in the center of the room and dismantled everything.

"I proposed the arrangement," he admitted, the truth bitter. "A strategic decision to secure your investment. But—" He hesitated. "Everything changed."

Andrew's expression remained skeptical. "Changed how?"

"I don't know," he said, the admission costing him more than he could calculate. His control was slipping, sliding away.

"Between lies and truth?" Andrew suggested, voice sharp.

"It started as an act but somewhere along the way it turned into…" He trailed off. "The engagement was fabricated. But what developed between us wasn't."

Andrew studied him in silence, assessing. Then he opened the contract folder, flipping through the pages until he found what he was looking for. His finger tapped a section of dense legal text.

"Do you recall clause 17.3 of our contract?" he asked, turning the folder so Ronan could see it. "The morality clause?"

Ronan's blood turned cold. It had been the one provision in the entire contract that had given him pause during the initial negotiations. Beauchamp's legal team had insisted on it and fighting it would have raised red flags. So, he'd instructed his own lawyers to let it pass without challenge.

"A provision allowing me to withdraw within 24 hours upon discovery of fraudulent or deceptive business practices," Andrew recited, not needing to look at the text. "Shall I read you the penalty provisions for a breach?"

"That won't be necessary." His mind computed the damage, which was fatal to Oath Capital in its current expansion phase. They'd leveraged on the promise of the Beauchamp capital.

Andrew's expression softened. "I don't want to invoke this clause. Despite what transpired, I believe in your vision for Oath Capital."

He knew better than to grasp at it—Negotiation 101. Let the other party continue, reveal their position.

"But I can't ignore what happened," Andrew continued. "My reputation, my investment philosophy—built on integrity.

How can I maintain this partnership after such a breach of trust?"

The question hung between them, rhetorical yet demanding an answer.

"You have until three tomorrow," Andrew said. "Twenty-four hours from when we signed. Convince me that there's truth here not only in your business model, but in the people behind it. Show me the man I thought I was investing in exists."

"I thought you invested in family men," Ronan said, a note of challenge in his voice. "Men with stability. With 'proper values.' I didn't think I could take that chance."

Andrew relaxed. "Is that what you thought? That I was looking for some perfect family picture?" He shook his head. "I don't invest in family men. I invest in whole men. Men who understand that business is about more than the bottom line." He sighed. "It was never about whether you were engaged. It was about seeing you capable of more than cold calculation."

He moved toward the door, then paused. "What disappoints me isn't the deception itself. It's that you thought you needed it. Your business stands on its own merits. But you couldn't trust that would be enough."

The accusation struck with accuracy. He had relied on controlling every variable. Trusting in the inherent value of what he'd built—trusting someone else to recognize it without manipulation—had seemed naïve.

When Andrew pulled open the door, the finality of his departure hung heavy in the air. "I'll be returning to Martha's Vineyard tonight. I'll send a car to your office at noon tomorrow to take you to the heliport," he said, his voice stripped of its usual charm. "We'll continue this discussion at my home before the deadline. I hope you'll give me reason not to proceed with withdrawal."

They parted without comment, leaving him alone in the

conference room, the finality sinking into his bones. For a long moment, he remained still. The company he'd built from nothing—his life's work—now teetered near complete ruin. Because of his refusal to trust in the value of what he'd created. Because of her moment of impulsive truth-telling.

When he emerged from the conference room, employees scattered as he approached, avoiding eye contact, focusing on their screens or paperwork. He strode through the open floor plan with measured steps, his face giving no hint of his thoughts, the storm inside hidden from view.

"Knox, Gabriel. My office. Now," he said, not breaking stride.

Once inside his office, he moved to the window.

Knox and Gabriel entered his office, closing the door behind them. For once, Knox's perpetual smirk was absent, replaced by grim concern.

"How bad?" Gabriel asked.

"Morality clause," he said, not turning from the window. "Twenty-four hours to convince Andrew not to withdraw."

"Jesus," Knox breathed. "The penalties would be—"

"Catastrophic," he finished for him, an edge of vulnerability in his voice. "Everything we've built."

A heavy silence filled the room. The three men who had built Oath Capital from the ground up now faced its potential ruin. This wasn't business—it was their life's work. Their legacy.

"What do we do?" Knox asked.

"I don't know," Ronan admitted, the words bitter on his lips. In all their years together, he'd never uttered those three words. He'd always had a plan, a strategy, a response to every challenge.

"She didn't know Andrew was there," Gabriel offered. "No one did."

His jaw tightened. "It doesn't change the outcome."

"So, what's our play?" Knox asked, leaning against the credenza. "How do we convince Andrew not to pull out?"

He moved to his desk, mind calculating likely scenarios, potential strategies. None of them seemed adequate for the situation.

"Andrew wants to see truth," he said. "Truth that isn't smoke and mirrors."

"And what would that be?" Gabriel asked.

The question hung in the air, unanswerable. He had built his career, his company, his entire life on precision and calculation. On knowing which move to make, which leverage to apply. This—this nebulous demand for authenticity—was outside his experience.

"I need to speak with her," he said.

Knox and Gabriel exchanged a look that he couldn't decipher.

"About that," Knox began, hesitation in his voice. "She left."

"Left where?" he asked.

"I don't know. She walked out," Gabriel said. "Took her purse and everything. Didn't say a word to anyone."

"And no one stopped her?" he asked. His voice had taken on a dangerous edge.

"After what happened?" Knox asked. "Everyone was too stunned to move."

Ronan turned to look at her desk—the same desk that had been positioned strategically within his line of sight since the day he'd hired her.

It was empty.

Not vacant—empty. The computer remained, but every personal item had vanished. The framed photograph of her grandmother that had sat beside her monitor. The small potted succulent she watered every Monday. The leather organizer embossed with her initials, a gift from the office on her birthday. Even her ridiculous bedazzled sunflower pen was gone from its spot in the ceramic holder.

His gaze dropped to his sunflowers in the trash can beside her desk.

Then a spark of light caught his eye—a small detail reflecting the overhead lighting.

There, in the center of her cleared desk, sat the cheap, gaudy sunflower ring. The fifteen-dollar piece of costume jewelry she'd spun an elaborate story around for the Beauchamps, explaining its sentimental value with such emotion that even he had believed it.

She'd left it.

She was gone.

He looked at the ring again. Cheap. Tacky. Yet seeing it abandoned like it had meant nothing hit harder than he wanted to admit.

"She's gone," he said again

Behind him, Knox and Gabriel didn't say anything.

Ronan stood there, staring at the empty desk.

———————————

Chapter 20

———————————

THE BOX WASN'T EVEN heavy.

She sat in the back of the taxi with everything she'd taken from Oath Capital in a small cardboard container resting on her knees.

Though she'd been his employee for six months, the past week had felt like a lifetime. That's how deeply she was invested—pouring herself into a role that now felt like ruins…

God, Ronan.

She'd never seen him look so blindsided.

The cab slowed.

"That'll be twenty-two fifty," the driver said as they pulled up outside of Flour & Honey.

She handed over her credit card. As she did, anxiety rolled through her. After today, she'd need to start watching every dollar. No more taxis. Back to the MetroCard.

She stepped onto the sidewalk, the weight of the box digging into her arms. The bakery's lights glowed warmly against the late afternoon sky. Her phone read 5:42 p.m. Through the window, she spotted Lucy behind the counter, wiping down surfaces.

The bell above the bakery door chimed as she stepped inside.

Lucy looked up.

"Dev? What's—" She stopped mid-sentence, taking in her expression—and the box in her arms. Realization set in. "Oh, honey," she said, coming around the counter. She glanced at the young woman boxing pastries. "Emma, can you hold things down for a bit? I need a few minutes with my friend."

Emma nodded.

Lucy guided her to a small table tucked into a corner, away from the last lingering customers. "Sit. I'll get us some tea."

Devney sank into the chair, every ounce of strength gone from her.

Lucy returned with two mismatched mugs. She set one down in front of Devney.

"I ruined everything," she said. "The deal. My job. Everything we worked for, gone."

Lucy slid a napkin across the table, then moved her chair closer, wrapping an arm around her shoulders as the sobs came —deep and wracking, held back for too long.

"They were talking about me," she said, twisting a napkin between her fingers. "The office. Whispering. Speculating. I kept catching people staring, then looking away when I noticed."

An expression shifted on Lucy's face. "And?"

"And I couldn't stand it," she said, her voice breaking. "After what we'd shared—the way he'd held me, made love to me, the things he'd whispered, hearing them reduce it to cheap office gossip…" She shook her head. "I snapped." She closed her eyes, the memory sharp as broken glass. "I stood in the middle of the office during the celebration and announced that we weren't engaged. That it was all a business strategy to secure the Beauchamp deal."

Lucy winced. "In front of everyone?"

"The entire room," she confirmed. "Including Andrew Beauchamp, who chose that exact moment to return for his phone."

"Oh, Dev." Lucy reached for her hand.

"You should have seen Ronan's face," she said through tears. "I've never seen him look like that." She wiped at her cheeks. "He trusted me."

Her voice broke again, fresh tears falling. "Why did I do that? What was I thinking?" The questions weren't for Lucy, but for herself. Questions she'd been asking since the moment she'd seen Andrew Beauchamp standing in the doorway.

"You couldn't have known Beauchamp would walk in at that exact moment."

"She shook her head. "I shouldn't have said anything."

She reached into the box and pulled out her bedazzled sunflower pen. "The most unprofessional thing on my desk. He used to look at it with this expression like he couldn't decide whether to be annoyed or amused."

Lucy took a sip of her tea. "You left? No confrontation? No explanation?" .

"I left the ring on my desk," she said. "It seemed like the right thing to do. When you walk away from someone you've..." She trailed off, unable to finish. "You leave the ring behind."

"But you paid for that ring," Lucy said clearly confused.

"I know. Stupid, right?" She twisted the pen between her fingers. "But it didn't feel like mine anymore."

"Because the feelings behind it became real?" Lucy asked.

She couldn't meet her friend's eyes. "Maybe. Not that it matters now. The worst part is that I meant what I told you yesterday. About my feelings for him."

"Why not tell him?" Lucy asked.

She gave a short, bitter laugh. "He'll never believe me."

"It was a mistake, Dev. An impulsive mistake."

"A mistake that might cost so many people their jobs." She closed her eyes, remembering the expansion plans, the new hires in process. "If Andrew withdraws, Oath Capital might not survive."

She looked toward the front window. "Those sunflowers he bought me. I threw them in the trash can by my desk."

A sympathetic look touched Lucy's eyes. "Why would you do that?"

"Because they felt like…" She searched for the words. "Like holding onto them would mean believing this could be fixed. And after what I did to him, to his company?" She shook her head. "Some things can't be undone. Better to accept it's over than torture myself with reminders of what might have been."

"Are you sure about that?" Lucy pressed. "Those sunflowers suggest otherwise."

"It doesn't matter now."

"What will you do now?" Lucy asked.

"I don't know. I can't use Oath Capital as a reference now. I exposed our fake engagement and destroyed a multi-million-dollar investment deal."

Despite everything, Lucy laughed. "Maybe leave that part off the resume."

Her phone buzzed in her pocket. Again. It had been vibrating since she left the office. She ignored it, as she'd ignored the previous calls.

"That's the sixth time," Lucy said, nodding toward the buzzing phone. "Aren't you going to check who it is?"

"It's him," she said with certainty. "Or Gabriel or Knox. It doesn't matter. What could I say to any of them?"

"Maybe 'I'm sorry?'" Lucy suggested. "It might be a start."

"*Sorry* doesn't fix this." She pulled the phone from her pocket, staring at the screen. Six missed calls. Four voice-mails.

Three text messages. All from him. "Sorry doesn't save a company from financial collapse."

Her finger hovered over the notification, tempted to hear his voice.

She turned the phone face down on the table.

"You can stay with me tonight," Lucy offered, recognizing her friend's exhaustion. "The guest room is ready."

"Thanks," she managed. "I don't think I could face my apartment right now. Too quiet. Too much time to think."

Lucy moved to the bakery kitchen, returning with a plate. "Emergency chocolate croissants," she announced, setting it down. "These were headed for the donation bin, but I warmed them up. Figured you needed them more. Because a sugar coma is exactly what this scenario calls for."

"Your solution to everything."

"Has it ever failed?" Lucy asked, pushing the plate closer. "Eat. Then we'll figure out what to do next."

The worst part wasn't the professional devastation. It was the realization that any chance of a real relationship with him was gone.

Lucy moved around the bakery with ease, boxing up the day's remaining pastries for her nightly donation drop-off. The display case sat mostly empty.

Devney stared at her phone again. The notifications had climbed. Seven missed calls. Five voice-mails. Four texts.

She picked it up, thumb hovering over the screen.

"Are you going to listen to them?" Lucy asked, glancing up from behind the counter.

"I can't."

"He deserves to hear from you, Dev. Even if it's to say goodbye."

"What would I even say?" Her voice was small. "'I'm sorry I destroyed everything you built because I couldn't handle office gossip?'"

"How about the truth?" Lucy said. "That you were hurt. That the subterfuge became too much. That somewhere along the way, fake started to feel a lot like the truth."

She shook her head. "He wouldn't understand. He doesn't do messy emotions. He does strategy. Planning. Control."

"Are you sure? Because the man I heard about wouldn't buy sunflowers for his assistant or make love to her like she was the most precious thing in the world."

The memory of their night together—the way he'd touched her with such reverence, whispered her name against her skin—hit her hard.

"It doesn't matter now. It's over."

"Is it? Because someone who's called eight times in three hours doesn't sound like someone who thinks it's over."

Her resolve wavered. What if Lucy was right? What if there was still a chance to explain, to apologize?

Her phone buzzed again. His name lit the screen for the eighth time.

"I can't talk to him," she whispered, silencing the call. "Not until I figure out what to do."

"And what exactly are you going to do?" Lucy asked, settling into the chair beside her.

Devney paused. He wasn't who she needed to apologize to. She looked up. "I need to go to Martha's Vineyard. I need to see the Beauchamps myself. To explain everything." She straightened in her chair, feeling as if there something she could do. "If Andrew hasn't pulled the deal yet, maybe there's still time to do something. This is my mess. I created it with my impulsive outburst, and now I need to fix it. I owe him that much."

"And if it doesn't work?" Lucy asked.

"Then at least I'll have tried," she said.

"How will you even get there?" Lucy asked. "It's not like you can grab a taxi to Martha's Vineyard."

"I don't know yet, but I'll figure it out. I have to."

Lucy gave her shoulders a squeeze. "Whatever happens, you'll face it. Then you'll move forward."

"How?" Devney asked.

"One step at a time," Lucy said. "The way we always do." She nodded.

As Lucy locked up Flour & Honey and led her upstairs to the apartment above, determination took root. This wasn't about salvaging a job. It was about doing what was right.

Inside, Lucy turned to her. "We'll figure out how to get you to the Vineyard in the morning."

Yes, they would, because she knew she had to make it right.

Chapter 21

HE HADN'T SLEPT.

The few hours he managed were fractured and useless, his thoughts returning again and again to the same empty feeling. So he did what he always did when everything else felt out of control—he went to the office. Early. Before the city had even begun to stir.

He'd tried to focus and failed.

Eventually, he left the stillness of his office.

Her desk sat like a monument untouched, unmoved, empty. Except for the ring.

That sunflower ring. Cheerful and her.

He'd called. He'd texted. Left voice-mails he didn't even remember recording. Eight calls.

Four texts. Five voice-mails. All unanswered.

He crossed the floor and picked the ring up.

The stones caught the morning light, throwing fractured rainbows across the surface of her desk. For a second, he stood there, staring at it, unable to move. She'd left it behind on purpose. A full stop at the end of whatever they were.

His fingers closed around it, and he slipped it into his pocket and turned toward the elevator.

He needed to talk to someone who understood people—not numbers. Someone who understood connection. He needed to talk to Eleanor Beauchamp.

He pulled out his phone as the elevator doors slid shut. "I need a charter," he said when the operator picked up.

"Yes, Mr. Wilder. Your flight to Martha's Vineyard is scheduled—"

"I'm moving it up."

"To when?" the operator asked.

"Now."

A pause.

"Now, sir?" the operator asked.

"I'll pay anything. I want wheels up in forty minutes." He ended the call.

Thirty minutes later the helicopter cut through the morning air, skimming over the Atlantic. Inside the cabin, he watched the coastline recede, Manhattan's skyline shrinking until it was a jagged line on the horizon—the distance that now stretched between his old life and whatever came next.

When the island eventually appeared in the distance—a crescent of green rising from the sea—he tried to order his thoughts. What could Eleanor possibly tell him that would salvage this situation? He didn't know. A rare thing, he was acting on impulse rather than calculation. The realization should have terrified him. Instead, it felt like relief.

The helicopter descended toward the clearing, the helipad tucked between wind-stirred trees and a narrow path that disappeared into the greenery. He didn't register much beyond that—only the hush of the blades slowing, the looming presence beyond the trees, and the certainty that there was no turning back.

A figure emerged onto the wide veranda, shielding their

eyes against the morning glare. Eleanor Beauchamp, elegant in white linen pants and a pale blue blouse.

She waited as he crossed the lawn. "Ronan," she said as he reached the porch. "You're quite early."

"Mrs. Beauchamp." He hesitated at the bottom stair. "I apologize for the intrusion."

"Eleanor, please." She gestured to the chair beside her. "And it's not an intrusion. Though I'm curious what brings you here at this hour. Andrew isn't expected back until before your scheduled meeting."

He took the offered seat, the wicker creaking beneath him. "That's fortunate. I was hoping to speak with you."

Her expression changed, subtle but assessing. "You don't look like you've slept at all."

"I haven't."

"How about some coffee?" she asked. "And perhaps some breakfast?"

"Coffee, yes. Breakfast might be ambitious."

She signaled to someone inside the house. Moments later, a staff member appeared, carrying a silver tray with coffee and pastries.

"Now," Eleanor said once they were alone again, passing him a steaming cup, "why are you here?"

He stared into the dark liquid, searching for the right words. How to explain what he barely understood himself.

"I've lost her," he said, the words emerging with unexpected honesty.

Eleanor didn't pretend to misunderstand. "Devney."

"Yes."

"And you believe I can help you win her back?" Eleanor's voice held a tone both wry and sincere.

"I don't know," he admitted. "I don't know what I expect you to tell me. I only know that you and Andrew have been married for forty years, and when he speaks of you, there's an emotion I never thought I wanted. Until now."

Sympathy passed over Eleanor's expression. She took a sip of her coffee, giving him a moment to collect himself.

"My husband believes the misrepresentation surrounding your engagement is the reason he should withdraw his investment," she said. "Is that correct?"

"Yes."

"But that's not why you're here, is it? You're not here to save the deal."

He met her gaze. "No. The deal means nothing if I can't fix what I broke with her."

Eleanor nodded "Tell me about her."

"She's…" He paused, searching for words adequate to describe her. "She challenges me. Questions me. Makes me see things differently." He looked down at his hands. "When we were together, she made me feel like I was someone worth knowing beyond the boardroom." He looked back up at Eleanor. "She has this ridiculous pen—covered in rhinestones, shaped like a sunflower. I should have told her to get rid of it, but I didn't. Because every time she used it, she'd glance at me, as if daring me to say what was on my mind. And I looked forward to those moments."

Eleanor studied him for a beat. "And the ring?" she asked.

He reached into his pocket and took out the ring. The metal held the heat of his body.

"I thought it was part of the act. A prop." He paused, thumb brushing over one of the glass petals. "But then she told the story at the gala. About her grandmother's sunflower garden. That was the first time I realized it meant more to her."

Eleanor remained silent, her eyes fixed on him as he turned the ring in his fingers.

"She left it on her desk when she walked out yesterday." He studied the band, rotating it slowly. "A clear message."

Eleanor took a long drink of her coffee before responding. "You know, when I met Andrew, he was much like you. Driven. Focused. Shrewd. He saw our relationship as a merger of compatible assets rather than a union of hearts."

He looked up. The Beauchamps had always seemed the picture of marital harmony.

"Oh yes," Eleanor continued, noting his expression. "He arranged our first meetings with the romantic spontaneity of a board presentation. Background checks. Character references. A complete dossier on my family connections and social standing."

"What changed?"

"I walked away." Eleanor set down her cup with a decisive click. "I told him I wouldn't be another acquisition, another item on his balance sheet of success. That if he wanted me, he would need to see me as a partner, not an asset."

He absorbed this, connecting it to Andrew's words in the conference room. *I don't invest in family men. I invest in whole men.*

"How did he respond?" he asked.

"Not well, at first. He made an interesting case—logic, timing, long-term compatibility. Synergy, as you business types like to call it. When I said no, he got annoyed. Then he went silent. And eventually, he realized he was heartbroken."

"And then?" he asked.

"And then he showed up at my father's summer house in Newport with nothing but the clothes on his back and a bouquet he'd picked from the roadside. No plan. No presentation. Himself, open and authentic for perhaps the first time in his life." Her eyes grew distant with the memory. "He said he'd rather have me without a plan than all the success in the world with one." She studied him over the rim of her cup. "He recognized a part of his younger self in you, I suspect. And hoped your Devney might do for you what I did for him."

He fell silent, turning her words over in his mind. The sunflower ring felt heavy in his palm. "I don't know how to fix this," he said. "I betrayed her trust. Used her in a scheme after she'd given me everything. And when it blew up, she was the one standing in the center of the explosion."

"Perhaps the question isn't how to fix it, but whether you're willing to risk having no plan at all." Eleanor's keen eyes missed nothing. "Whether you're willing to stand before her with no strategy, no calculation, nothing but the truth of what you feel."

"And if that's not enough?" he asked.

"Then at least you'll have been honest. With her, and with yourself." Eleanor reached over and closed his fingers around the ring. "That's the only foundation worth building on. Take it from someone who knows."

The only sounds were the distant crash of waves against the shore and the call of gulls overhead. He felt some of the tightness inside him ease for the first time in days, maybe even longer. Because he had finally asked the right questions of the right person.

"Thank you," he said, rising from his chair. "You've given me a great deal to think about."

Eleanor gestured toward the house. "Andrew will be back soon. You might want to freshen up before your meeting. There's a guest room prepared for you inside."

He nodded, slipping the ring back into his pocket. As he turned to go, Eleanor spoke again.

"Ronan."

He paused, looking back.

"Sometimes the most successful negotiations are the ones where you're willing to lose everything for the right reason."

Later, he stood in Andrew Beauchamp's study, watching the

older man read through the documents he'd presented. The room exuded old money and power and the subtle scent of success.

Andrew looked up, setting the papers aside. "This is your proposal? To restructure the entire deal?"

"Yes." He maintained eye contact.

"These terms are less favorable to Oath Capital than our original agreement."

"Yes."

"You're offering me a larger stake for the same investment, with greater board representation and a stronger morality clause." Andrew eyed him with interest. "Why?"

"Because it's the offer I should have made from the beginning, based on the merits of the business, not on false impressions or manipulations."

"And your investors will accept these terms? Your board?"

"They'll have to." He met Andrew's gaze. "It's my company. My decision."

Andrew's mouth twitched, the gesture unreadable. "Even if it costs you personal equity?"

"Even then."

He tapped the papers, slow and measured. "My wife tells me you arrived early today. That you spent some time in her company."

"I did."

"Eleanor has always been an excellent judge of character." Andrew's tone was even, though his eyes told a different story. "She sees things I sometimes miss."

He waited, sensing there was more.

"She believes you've learned a valuable lesson from this situation."

"I have."

"May I ask what?"

"That authentic connection is worth more than strategic

advantage. That being seen—truly seen—by the right person changes everything." He paused, feeling his way toward a truth he was beginning to understand. "That I've spent my life building an empire at the expense of building a life."

Andrew nodded, as if he had confirmed an important truth. "And Ms. Sinclair? Where does she fit into this new understanding?"

"She's essential to it," he admitted. "But I may have realized that too late."

"Have you?" Andrew rose from his desk and moved to the window, looking out over the grounds sloping down to the ocean. "I've found, over a lifetime in business, that it's rarely too late to correct a mistake, provided one is willing to pay the full price of the correction."

"I am."

Andrew turned from the window, approval in his expression. "Then I believe we have a deal, Ronan." He extended his hand. "The revised terms are acceptable."

He felt a sudden, immense relief as they shook hands. One crisis averted. But the one that mattered most remained unresolved.

"Thank you," he said, gathering the signed documents. "Oath Capital will honor your trust."

"My security alerted me through text that Ms. Sinclair arrived some time ago," Andrew said. "Rather determined to speak with me. Eleanor's been keeping her company while we finished here."

His breath caught. "Devney?"

Andrew nodded. "Apparently she is quite distraught, by all appearances. Said she needed to make things right." He paused. "Eleanor is rather taken with her. She recognizes a kindred spirit."

He was already moving toward the door, his pulse pounding. "Where did you say they were?" he asked.

"Eastern veranda. Through the main hall, past the library, then right at the—"

But Ronan was gone, striding through the house with singular focus. All he could think was that she was here. He rounded the corner past the library, sunlight streaming through tall windows. Another turn, and the eastern veranda came into view through the French doors—a wide, covered porch that looked out over the formal garden and the sea beyond.

And there, seated in wicker chairs angled toward the ocean, were two women. Eleanor, composed and serene. And beside her—Devney. He recognized her instantly, even from behind. The ponytail. The gentle slope of her shoulders. The tension in her posture, like she couldn't quite let herself relax, even here. She still wore the same clothes from yesterday.

As if sensing his presence, she turned—enough that he caught a glimpse of her profile.

Even that was enough to see the exhaustion in her expression.

He moved toward the doors, hand reaching for the handle—

And paused as a hand touched his arm.

Andrew stood beside him, having followed from the study. "Give them time," he said, his gaze moving between Ronan and the women on the veranda. "Some conversations need to reach their natural conclusion."

He wanted to protest, to push past him and rush to her side. To demand explanations, to offer apologies, to say all the things that had been burning inside him since she'd walked out. But an unspoken message in Andrew's expression gave him pause.

"What is she doing here?" he asked.

"The same thing you are, I imagine." Andrew's gaze held firm. "Trying to fix what matters most."

Through the glass, he watched as Eleanor reached across

the space between the chairs to take Devney's hand. Whatever Eleanor said made her tense shoulders relax, her head nod in apparent agreement.

"They'll be finished soon," Andrew said. "We'll come back in a few minutes and check on them."

Ronan nodded, gaze still locked on the veranda. On her.

"Come," Andrew said, already turning. "While we wait, perhaps you can tell me more about your expansion plans."

He hesitated. And maybe Andrew was right. Maybe this was the time to compose himself before the most important conversation of his life.

Chapter 22

"HE WON'T FORGIVE ME," she said, her voice barely louder than the breeze rustling through the sea grass. "I destroyed everything."

Eleanor Beauchamp studied her from the adjacent wicker chair, the ocean breeze ruffling her silver hair. "You give yourself too much credit, my dear. And him too little."

The Beauchamp estate stretched before them, manicured gardens cascading down to a private beach. So different from her cramped Brooklyn apartment or the crowded streets of Manhattan. A different world. One where people like her didn't belong.

"I stood there with the entire office watching, your husband included, and announced our engagement was fake. A business strategy. A lie. I betrayed his trust."

"Yes, you did," Eleanor agreed, her bluntness startling. "But the question isn't whether you made a mistake. We all do that. The question is why you're here."

She turned to face her host, struck by the directness of Eleanor's gaze. No judgment, but no coddling either.

"I want to fix it. The deal, at least. The company. Those people don't deserve to lose their jobs because of me."

"Only the company?" Eleanor asked, her eyes sharp with perception.

Heat crept up her neck. "What else could I hope to fix?" she asked.

"I think you know." Eleanor set her cup down on the small table between them. "Otherwise, you wouldn't have come all this way."

Devney glanced away, her gaze skimming the horizon. The trip had been exhausting—a pre-dawn bus to Woods Hole, the morning ferry to the Vineyard, then an overpriced taxi across the island.

"I love him," she admitted, the words spilling out. "I didn't plan to. It was supposed to be a business arrangement. A fake engagement to secure your husband's investment. But somewhere along the way love happened."

"The pretend became real," Eleanor said.

"Yes." She twisted her hands in her lap, feeling strangely naked without the ring she'd left behind. "But that doesn't matter now. He'll never trust me again. And I don't blame him."

Eleanor leaned back, hands resting in her lap, expression distant as the breeze played with the loose strands of her hair.

"Let me tell you a story," Eleanor said. One I've never told anyone." Her gaze drifted toward the horizon, the distant waves reflected in her eyes. "Not even Andrew."Devney sat up, curious.

"When I was younger," Eleanor began, her voice hushed, "I was infatuated with a man named Charles Whitmore." A small, quiet laugh escaped her. "He was handsome. Charming. He always knew exactly what to say and when to say it. And I…" She shook her head. "I was young enough to believe that words were the truest reflection of a person."

Devney tilted her head. "What happened?"

Eleanor's focus stayed on the water. "Charles made me feel like the center of his universe when he spoke. But words are easy. What I didn't notice—what I didn't know how to look for—were the things he *didn't* say."

She leaned in. "The things he didn't say?"

The older woman nodded slowly, still watching the tide roll in. "Yes. Like how he never asked how my day had been when I was quiet. Or how he never noticed when I was cold and didn't offer his coat. He'd plan grand dates, dazzling affairs meant to impress, but he never remembered that I hated oysters or I preferred tea over coffee.

"He showed me exactly who he was, but I wasn't paying attention. I was young," Eleanor said, finally turning back. "And I mistook the noise for substance. I thought love was about the big moments, the declarations, the grand gestures. But it's not."

Her voice dropped, certain now. "Love is in the quiet things. The unspoken acts. The small details you notice."

Devney thought of Ronan.

Eleanor's hands settled in her lap, her voice kind. "Like how Andrew always refills my teacup before I realize it's empty. Or how he used to fix the loose hinge on the kitchen cabinet without saying a word because he knew it annoyed me." A gentler light came into her eyes. "Or how he noticed—before I ever did—that my favorite perfume was running low and ordered another bottle."

Devney thought back to moments with Ronan. The way he adjusted the thermostat in his office when he noticed her shiver. The sunflowers he brought after she mentioned her grandmother's garden. The way he always made sure her favorite sparkling water was stocked in the office fridge. Little things, like how she liked her coffee. The quiet things. Things that spoke louder than words ever could.

"Men don't always tell you what matters," Eleanor said. "But they show you. In ways they don't even realize."

Her throat was tight now. She had lost him and she was devastated.

Eleanor's hand covered hers, the touch cool and grounding. "You want to know how he feels? Pay attention to what he does when no one's watching. To the way he reacts when you're silent. To the things he remembers that you never expected him to. That's where love lives. In the spaces between the words."

Tears stung her eyes as memories rushed back—not of the deliberate moves he had made to secure the deal, but of the unguarded moments when he'd shown her a real part of himself. The way he looked at her when he thought she wasn't paying attention. The vulnerability he'd tried so hard to hide but couldn't quite keep from slipping through.

"You and he," Eleanor continued, her tone quiet but firm, "are both so busy protecting yourselves. Tell him how you feel."

"But what if I'm too late?" Her voice was barely above a whisper. "What if he doesn't believe me? What if my words aren't enough?"

"Then show him. Men may not always speak their hearts, but they notice when you do."

The words settled deep, igniting hope that was fragile but fierce. Because maybe it wasn't too late. She wiped her eyes and looked back toward the house, not expecting anything— just needing a moment to breathe.

"I should have told him sooner," she said softly. "About how I felt."

Eleanor didn't answer right away. Then, gently, "You're not the only one who came today."

Devney stilled. "He's here?"

"Yes. We had quite an illuminating conversation."

"And you didn't think to tell me?"

"You needed time to figure out what you really came here for."

"I—" Her throat tightened, words tangling with emotion. "Why would you let me sit here when he was so close?"

"Because, my dear," came the reply, "sometimes the hardest truths need space to settle. And sometimes…" Her gaze drifted toward the door where he had disappeared, "they need the right moment to be heard."

"You talked to him?"

The older woman's eyes sharpened with understanding. "Yes. About mistakes. About trust. About what truly matters when empires crumble." She patted Devney's hand. "He'll find you when he's ready," Eleanor said. "Andrew will keep him occupied for now."

The realization that they had both traveled to this place, seemingly drawn by the same unseen connection, felt impossible—too coincidental to be mere chance.

"Why would he come here?"

"Perhaps because some things are too important to leave unfinished. You both came seeking answers. Maybe it was for the same question."

Eleanor rose from her chair. "Now, I believe I'll go check on the men. Business negotiations can make Andrew irritable if they drag on too long."

"Wait—" Panic seized her. "What should I say to him? I came all this way to talk to Andrew. I have no idea what to tell Ronan."

"The truth, my dear. It's the only thing worth building on." Then she was gone, leaving Devney alone with the crash of waves and a decision to make.

The truth was simple, but saying it felt terrifying. That she had fallen in love with him during their charade.

But the deepest truth—the one that had pushed her across

the sound on a crowded ferry and through the winding streets of the island in an overpriced taxi—was that she couldn't live with having walked away. Couldn't bear the thought of leaving him to deal with the fallout alone. She created the mess. She had to be the one to try to fix it.

A sound behind her made her turn. The French doors swung open, and there he stood. He looked tired. The lines of his suit rumpled, his hair mussed as if he'd run his hands through it countless times. Dark circles shadowed his eyes— eyes that fixed on her with an intensity that made her breath catch.

She stood, ready to face him.

Neither spoke as he crossed the veranda to stand before her, close enough that she could catch the scent of his cologne, see the tension in his jaw, the pulse beating at his throat.

"You're here," he said, his voice low and trembling with emotion.

Two words. One heartbeat.

"Yes. I came to fix what I broke. The deal. The company." She paused. "Your trust."

"How did you get here?" he asked. The question seemed oddly important to him.

"Ferry. Then taxi." She gestured vaguely toward the island. "It took a while, but I made it."

A muscle twitched in his jaw. "You crossed the sound. On the ferry."

"It wasn't that bad." A lie. The trip had been a blur— anxious hours spent staring at the horizon, her mind racing with every outcome, her heart pounding louder with each passing mile.

"Why?" he asked.

The moment stretched between them, thick with possibility and fear. Eleanor's words echoed in her mind. The truth. It's the only thing worth building on.

He took a step closer, his voice low and intense. "The deception was mine, Devney. From the beginning. I created this mess because I didn't trust my own work—or you—to be enough. I put you in an impossible position."

"And I broke your trust to protect my pride. I was so scared of what people would think, of them cheapening what felt so real."

"Devney…" His voice cracked, raw and vulnerable.

"I kept going with the charade because I was falling in love with you."

His look gave her hope.

"Not just with the idea of you, but with the man who held me like I was precious, who whispered my name in the dark."

His composure slipped for a second. He reached into his pocket and pulled out the ring.

"You kept it," she whispered.

"I thought it was a message. That you were severing the connection between us. Ending the charade."

"It was." Her eyes burned with unshed tears. "I thought that's what you wanted. What you needed. After I ruined everything."

"What I need is you. All of you."

The moment hung suspended between them—a heartbeat of time in which everything might change, or nothing at all.

"I love you." Her heart laid bare. "Not the CEO. Not the man with the perfect plan. You. The man who brought me sunflowers because I once mentioned my grandmother's garden. The man who tolerates my ridiculous pen because he knows it matters to me. The man who looks at me like…like I matter."

"You do." His voice was barely above a whisper, but the power of those two words settled deep inside. "And you didn't ruin everything."

"The deal—"

"Is secure." He held up a hand to stop her. "Andrew and I reached an agreement. Different terms. More favorable to him. But the company will survive."

Relief crashed through her, so powerful she swayed on her feet. "So, my coming here—"

"—might have started as business," he said, closing the distance between them, his free hand lifting to cup her cheek, "but somewhere along the way, it became about us."

His touch sent electricity through her, heat sinking into her bones. "I don't understand." Her voice was barely a whisper.

"I came here this morning to talk to Eleanor," he admitted, his thumb brushing across her cheekbone. "To ask her how to get you back."

The confession stole her breath. "Why would you want that? After what I did?" she asked.

"Because, fake or not, these past weeks with you have been the most real thing in my life." His eyes held hers, vulnerability replacing the control she had always associated with him. "The sunflowers weren't strategy. The moments in my office, the night we spent together—none of that was for Andrew Beauchamp's business."

"Then what was it for?" she asked.

"For this." He pressed the ring into her palm, closing her fingers around it. "A foundation. One worth building on. If you'll help me."

She searched his face, looking for any trace of strategy, but all she found was raw honesty—a man without a plan, offering nothing but himself.

"I'm not good at this," he admitted, his voice low. "At vulnerability. At trust. At forgiveness. But I want to learn. With you."

Tears spilled down her cheeks, unchecked. "What if I mess up again? What if my impulsiveness—"

"Then we'll fix it. Together." His hand slid into her hair,

drawing her closer. "No more charades. No more strategic advantages. Only us. Figuring it out as we go."

The ring pressed into her palm, still holding the heat from his pocket. Not a symbol of the ruse any longer, but of possibility. Of a beginning built on truth rather than strategy.

"Together," she echoed, the word a promise, a hope—a future she hadn't dared imagine twenty-four hours ago.

And then his lips found hers, and no more words were necessary.

Chapter 23

THE MANHATTAN SKYLINE SPREAD before him as he stood in his kitchen, taking in the view. Three days had passed since Martha's Vineyard—three days of conversations stretching into the night, of rediscovered laughter, of plans made and unmade. Three days of finding their footing on new ground.

Today, they would return to Oath Capital together. Not as boss and assistant engaged in an elaborate charade, but as two people choosing to build a life from the wreckage of what had broken.

His phone buzzed on the counter.

DEVNEY: On my way. Bringing coffee from that place on 3rd you pretend not to like. Your kitchen remains tragically understocked. Don't argue.

RONAN: I wouldn't dream of it.

Fifteen minutes later, the elevator's chime announced her arrival, then she appeared in the kitchen doorway, golden hair loose around her shoulders, a cardboard drink carrier in one hand and a brown paper bag in the other.

"Your breakfast delivery has arrived," she announced, her tone triumphant, chasing the morning hush from the room. "Fresh coffee and croissants, because life's too short for stale bagels."

"Is that so?" he asked, accepting the bag she thrust toward him. Their fingers brushed in the exchange, sending a current of awareness through him that he no longer tried to suppress.

"Absolutely. You don't do anything halfway, Ronan Wilder." She moved to the cupboard where she knew his plates were kept. "Including breakfast."

He watched her navigate his kitchen with ease, setting out plates and butter, arranging the flaky pastries like she'd done it a hundred times before. The domesticity of the scene struck him hard—how she had slipped into the empty spaces of his life, filling them with color and movement and sound. How natural it felt to wake up with her beside him, to share coffee and quiet morning conversation after the passion of the night before.

"Are you nervous?" he asked, as she arranged their breakfast on the island between them.

"About walking into Oath Capital after my dramatic exit? About facing an office full of people who witnessed the entire debacle?" She released a shaky breath. "*Terrified* would be more accurate."

"We don't have to do this today," he said, reaching across the counter to take her hand. "The company will survive another day without us."

Her fingers tightened around his, her eyes meeting his, clear and unwavering. "Yes, we do. The longer we wait, the harder it becomes. Besides," she added, "I've never been good at backing down from a challenge."

"No," he agreed. "It's one of your most infuriating qualities."

"You find me infuriating?" she asked, her tone light.

He circled the island to stand before her, close enough to feel the warmth that always seemed to radiate from her—now inextricably tied to memories of her fingers in his hair as the fever ravaged him, of her in his kitchen making soup, of her dressed in his T-shirt.

"Infuriating," he confirmed, his voice dropping to a whisper as he tucked a strand of hair behind her ear. "Challenging. Essential."

The slight catch in her breathing sent satisfaction coursing through him. For a man who had built an empire on his ability to read markets and predict outcomes, discovering the impact of his touch, his words on this woman, felt like the most valuable intelligence he'd gathered.

"We should eat," she said, though she made no move to step away. "Before the croissants get cold."

"Yes," he agreed, reluctant to break the moment. "Can't have cold croissants."

They ate in comfortable silence for a few moments before she spoke again.

"Have you decided what we're going to tell everyone?" she asked, her voice casual.

"The truth," he said. "That the relationship is real."

"Simple and direct."

"They don't need any more," he said firmly.

"And HR? I mean, there are policies in place."

"About the CEO dating his assistant?" he asked. "I'm the CEO, Devney. I make the policies."

She opened her mouth as if to protest, then shut it again, a short laugh escaping instead. "Well, when you put it that way."

"Your position and value to the company remain unchanged," he continued, his tone shedding its formal edge. "You've earned your place at Oath Capital through your own merit. We'll make whatever adjustments are necessary, but I won't shuffle you off to another department to make things neater on paper."

"I'm glad," she said, relief clear in her tone. "I'd hate to work for Gabriel. He color-codes his emails by urgency."

"A man after my own heart," he said dryly, though his lips twitched.

"Terrifying," she said, but her eyes sparkled. She reached across the counter, her fingers finding his with unerring precision. "I'm glad I get to stay where I belong."

"With me," he said, the words both statement and question.

"With you," she confirmed.

The rest of breakfast passed in a haze of plans and contingencies—habit for him, necessity for her. By the time they stepped into the elevator that would carry them to the garage, a strange calm had settled over him. Whatever happened at Oath Capital today, they would face it together.

The drive to the office passed in silence, each lost in their own thoughts as Manhattan streamed past the windows. When they pulled into the executive parking garage, he cut the engine but made no move to exit the car.

"Are you having second thoughts?" she asked.

"No," he said, struck by how true that was. He searched for the words, unusual for someone who usually had them ready. "Centering myself."

She said nothing, responding with a single nod. "That seems to be our specialty lately."

The elevator ride felt longer than usual, the air between them charged with anticipation. When the doors slid open, revealing the expansive glass and chrome of Oath Capital, he did what he had never done before.

He reached for her hand.

The gesture was small—fingers intertwined, palms pressed —but its significance was not lost on either of them. Or he noted with a trace of grim irony, on the wide-eyed receptionist who nearly dropped her phone at the sight.

"Let the games begin," she murmured, her grip tightening before she stepped forward with the confidence that had first caught his attention all those months ago.

They moved through the office together, aware of the ripple effect their arrival created. Conversations halted mid-sentence. Heads turned. Eyes widened. The whispers followed, low and immediate, trailing in their wake.

"Devney!" Julia from Accounting stood abruptly from her desk, her expression shifting from shock to intrigue, then to sudden understanding that widened her eyes as her gaze dropped to their joined hands. "You're back!"

"I am," she confirmed, her voice level despite the tremor he felt through their connected palms.

"And you're…" Julia's eyes widened, darting between them with unabashed interest.

"Together," he said, his tone firm enough to discourage further questions but not harsh enough to silence them.

The single word sent a fresh wave of whispers rippling through the office. He felt Devney's posture straighten beside him, her chin lifting in that familiar, stubborn way.

"I believe you all have work to do," he reminded the gathered employees, though without the cutting edge his voice usually carried in such moments. "The quarterly reports won't complete themselves."

The office returned to work, though whispers of speculation continued. He led her to her desk, which had remained untouched since her departure—the computer and phone waiting in silence.

She paused, her fingers brushing the spot where the

sunflower ring had rested—no longer on her hand, but vivid in her mind.

"I half-expected someone else to be sitting here by now," she murmured.

He shook his head, amusement crossing his face. "No one would dare."

"Because you told them not to?" she asked.

"Because I didn't need to."

She turned to look at him.

He met her gaze without flinching. "You're irreplaceable."

The words landed between them—simple, direct, and far more vulnerable than anything he'd said the week before. And she felt it, to her bones.

Their moment was interrupted by the arrival of Knox and Gabriel, both looking uncharacteristically solemn as they approached. Knox's usual smirk was absent, replaced by concern, while Gabriel's expression offered no clues.

"Morning meeting in five," Gabriel said, his gaze dropping to their joined hands before settling back on Ronan. "The team needs to hear about the new Beauchamp terms from you."

He nodded, grateful for the normalcy of business operations. No board meetings, no rumors—nothing but the day-to-day rhythm of the company he'd built. "We'll be there."

"Welcome back, Sunshine," Knox said to her, his knowing smile making an appearance. "The place has been gloomier without you."

"Thanks, Knox," she said, her posture easing as if a weight had been set down. "It's good to be back."

The two men departed, Knox whispering something to Gabriel that made the stoic man's lips twitch.

"They seem different," she observed once they were alone.

"They are," he agreed. "We all are."

He turned to face her, aware of the curious eyes that still

watched them from around the office, but finding himself strangely unconcerned by the scrutiny. Eleanor Beauchamp's words echoed in his mind: *Sometimes the most successful negotiations are the ones where you're willing to lose everything for the right reasons.*

"Before we go in there," he said, taking both her hands in his, "I need you to know this."

She tilted her head, waiting. No impatient interjection, no nervous chatter. Only her presence—which he had come to value more than his previous calculations allowed for.

"Whatever happens today, however the office reacts, it doesn't change this." He lifted their joined hands. "Us. I meant what I said on Martha's Vineyard. I'm all in, Devney. No more charades. No more strategies."

"So am I." She squeezed his hands, the gesture conveying strength rather than seeking it. "Now let's go face the music together."

As they walked toward the meeting room, a new certainty settled—grounded and real. Not the scripted confidence of a business strategy, but the quiet strength of what was truly built to last. What was real.

Together, they pushed open the meeting room doors to face whatever awaited them on the other side.

Chapter 24

WHEN THE ELEVATOR doors slid open the next morning, her senses were flooded with color. Sunflowers. Dozens of them. Bright yellow blooms split between several crystal vases, all arranged across her desk like they were eagerly awaiting her arrival. Behind this sea of gold and green stood Ronan, an expression of self-satisfaction on his face. His hands were tucked into the pockets of his flawlessly tailored suit, as if he hadn't turned her workspace into a botanical display.

"Good morning," he said, his voice carrying that tone that made her heart skip.

"Good morning," she said as she crossed the room. "I see you've been busy."

"I have excellent time management skills," Ronan said, the corner of his mouth lifting in that almost-smile she'd grown to cherish. "The florist opens at six."

She reached out to touch one of the velvet petals, her other hand instinctively moving to the pocket of her blazer where she'd slipped the key he'd given her yesterday—the key attached to a small silver sunflower charm. The thoughtfulness of it all—the flowers, the key, the way he'd remembered every detail that mattered to her—left her momentarily speechless.

"You're staring," Ronan observed, breaking into her thoughts.

"I'm appreciating the view," she murmured, setting down her bag and stepping closer to him.

"The flowers or me?" he asked, and there it was again—that playfulness that still caught her off guard.

"Both." She straightened his already-perfect tie, letting her fingers linger. "But mostly you."

His eyes darkened, his gaze dropping to her lips before reluctantly pulling away. "We should establish some workplace boundaries," he murmured, though the regret in his tone suggested he wasn't entirely sold on the idea.

"Probably," she agreed, stepping back with exaggerated professionalism. "Very wise, Mr. Wilder."

"Don't start," he warned, though the shift at the corner of his mouth gave him away. "I have a reputation to maintain."

"Of course." She nodded. "The fearsome CEO. The financial mastermind. The one who reduced an intern to tears over a misaligned spreadsheet."

"That was one time," he protested, looking adorably defensive.

She laughed, the sound drawing curious glances from employees passing by. The office was still adjusting to this new version of Ronan Wilder—one with edges that didn't cut so sharply, one who lingered instead of retreating. It was a far cry from the icy, unapproachable figure they'd all come to fear. Now they were witnessing a far more unsettling development: Ronan Wilder, in love.

"I have meetings until two," he said, checking his watch with barely concealed reluctance. "Dinner tonight?"

"I'd like that," she replied. "But I promised Lucy I'd stop by the bakery after work. I haven't seen her since—"

"Since before my last trip to Martha's Vineyard," he finished, the stern lines around his eyes seeming to ease. "You should go. She'll want details."

"Oh, she'll demand them," she said with a grin. "Along with a full character assessment of you."

"Should I be worried?" he asked, only half-joking.

"Absolutely terrified."

He laughed—a real, unrestrained laugh that transformed his face and sent a ripple of whispers across the office. Ronan Wilder, laughing at 8:47 in the morning? The world had turned upside down.

"Well then, you enjoy some time," he said, backing toward his office with a lingering glance. "But how about I pick you both up at seven and join you for dinner?"

"That sounds great. I'll let her know. She's been waiting for this moment since I first mentioned your name."

He stepped in and pressed a quick kiss to her cheek.

"I'd better get to that meeting," he said, like he hadn't short-circuited her morning. And like that, he was gone.

THE MORNING SLIPPED by in a flurry of emails, meetings, and phone calls. But no matter how focused she tried to be, her eyes kept drifting to the sunflowers Ronan made sure were on her desk always. They were impossible to ignore—a bright, cheerful reminder that her life had changed in ways she was still trying to understand.

Julia from Accounting stopped by three times with increasingly flimsy excuses, each visit ending with a pointed glance at the flowers and a failed attempt at casual questioning.

By lunchtime, she'd fielded so many inquiries about her relationship status that she was understanding why Ronan preferred the sanctuary of his glass-walled office. Privacy was a precious commodity in the corporate fishbowl, especially when you were dating the CEO.

Dating. The word still felt strange—inadequate for what had bloomed between them during those moments of pretending and discovery. They were beyond dating, though not at the stage the fake engagement had suggested. They existed in some undefined space between, finding their footing in reality after so long in fiction.

Her phone buzzed as she finished her salad at her desk.

LUCY: Flour delivery running late. Might need to push back our dinner by 30 mins. Still coming, right? I need DETAILS.

She smiled and typed back.

DEVNEY: Wouldn't miss it. And prepare yourself. Ronan's joining us. He'll meet us at the bakery at 7:00.

The typing dots appeared. Vanished. Returned.

LUCY: WHAT?! The ice king cometh to my humble bakery? Am I allowed to ask inappropriate questions?

DEVNEY: Within reason.

Devney pictured Ronan's face when confronted with Lucy's unfiltered curiosity.

DEVNEY: Go easy on him. He's still new to all this.

LUCY: No promises. See you tonight.

THE AFTERNOON CRAWLED BY, her anticipation growing with each passing hour. Not for Lucy's reaction to Ronan, but for this next step in their relationship—introducing him to the most important person in her life. It felt like blending two worlds that had existed in parallel until now, and she wondered if bringing them together would be awkward.

At exactly 5:45, she gathered her things and stopped by Ronan's office. He was on the phone, his brow furrowed in concentration, but the focused intensity in his face gave way to a warmer look the moment he spotted her in the doorway. She gestured she was heading out, not wanting to interrupt what looked like an important call.

Without warning, Ronan held up a finger—wordlessly asking her to wait—then turned back to his call.

"Davis, I need to put you on hold." He pressed a button on his phone and crossed to where she stood.

"Heading to meet Lucy?" he asked, his tone quieter now, the sharp edge of command gone.

"Yes," she replied, still a little thrown by how he could switch between corporate shark and attentive boyfriend. "Did you put Tokyo on hold?"

"Tokyo can wait," he said, and while her mind raced to catch up, he leaned down and kissed her—right there in the doorway of his glass-walled office. It was brief but undeniably deliberate. His hand cupped her cheek with affection from him that she hadn't anticipated.

When he pulled back, his eyes held hers with intensity. "I'll see you at the bakery at seven."

"Okay," she managed, momentarily speechless at this public display of affection from a man who meticulously managed every aspect of his professional image.

Knox appeared beside them, his expression clearly surprised. "Well," he drawled, looking between them with a grin that said he'd seen what he needed to. "Guess that answers whether you two are keeping things professional at work."

Ronan leveled him with a glare that would have withered most employees on the spot, but Knox only grinned wider.

"Go," Ronan murmured, his thumb brushing her cheek once more before stepping back. "I'll finish this call and meet you there."

"Don't be late," she said, finding her voice at last.

Knox's laughter followed her to the elevator, a reminder that she wasn't the only one enjoying this new version of Ronan—the one who kissed her goodbye in full view of the office and put Tokyo on hold because she mattered more.

THE BELL ABOVE FLOUR & Honey's door chimed as Devney stepped inside. At the end of the day, a few stragglers lingered over their drinks near the window, the final notes of music playing beneath the hum of closing-time routines.

Lucy looked up from behind the counter, flour dusting her dark hair and a streak of what might have been chocolate smeared across one cheek. Her eyes widened at the sight of Devney, and she set down the tray she'd been wrapping.

"Finally!" she said, rounding the counter. "I was starting to think you'd gotten caught in Ronan's gravitational pull and would never escape."

"Very funny," Devney replied, accepting Lucy's floury hug. "Sorry I'm late. Things are still…adjusting at the office."

Lucy pulled back, her eyes narrowing as she studied Devney's face. "You're glowing," she accused, tilting her head with theatrical revulsion. "Like, actually glowing. It's disgusting."

Devney felt the heat rise to her cheeks. "Am not."

"Are too," Lucy said, steering them toward their usual table in the corner. "And you're blushing, which only confirms my theory that Ronan Wilder has thoroughly corrupted my pragmatic best friend into a romantic sap."

"I wouldn't go that far," Devney said, but the way her mouth twitched at the corners gave her away.

Lucy disappeared into the kitchen, returning with two steaming mugs of tea and a plate of madeleines. "So," she said, sliding into the chair across from Devney. "How's the office handling the news? Is HR having a collective aneurysm? Has Julia from Accounting started a gossip newsletter yet?"

Devney laughed. "The office is adjusting. Some people are still in shock. Others are weirdly supportive. Knox and Gabriel keep making these cryptic comments about winning bets."

"And Ronan?" Lucy pressed, leaning forward with unabashed interest. "How's Mr. Ice King handling public displays of affection in his buttoned-up corporate kingdom?"

The memory of his goodbye kiss in the doorway lingered, steady and sweet, like a secret she wasn't ready to let go. "Better than I expected, actually. He kissed me goodbye today. In his office doorway. In full view of everyone still there."

Lucy's jaw dropped. "No. Way."

"Yes way," Devney said, unable to keep the happiness from her voice. "And he sent my desk into floristry overload this morning. Sunflowers. Dozens of them."

"Okay, I'm officially swooning," Lucy said. "But I'm still reserving the right to interrogate him when he gets here."

"About that," Devney began, "he's joining us as soon as he finishes a call with Tokyo."

"Perfect," Lucy said, glancing at her watch. "That gives us about forty-five minutes for you to tell me everything that happened on Martha's Vineyard. I want details, Sinclair. Not the sanitized version you texted me."

"It wasn't sanitized," Devney protested.

"*'Things worked out. Coming home tomorrow.'* That was your entire text," Lucy deadpanned. "Now, start talking."

Devney took a deep breath and, between sips of tea and bites of madeleine, told her everything—the desperate journey to the island, her conversation with Eleanor, the shock of learning he was there too, and finally, their honest confessions on the veranda.

"When he said what he did. I didn't even know what to say," she said. "It felt like he was offering me back what I hadn't realized I'd been missing."

Lucy's eyes were suspiciously bright. "That's romantic for a man who probably color-codes his sock drawer."

"He does," Devney laughed. "But he's also much more than that. He's considerate and passionate and surprisingly vulnerable when he lets his guard down."

"And clearly in love with you," Lucy added, genuine emotion tempering her usual sharp wit.

"Yeah," Devney said, looking down into her mug. "I'm still getting used to that part."

"Tell me the truth. How was it really at the office? Really?" Lucy asked, her voice growing more serious. "I know you're putting on a brave face, but walking back in there after what happened…"

Devney sobered, cradling her mug between her hands. "It wasn't easy," she admitted. "There were a lot of stares, whispers. But Ronan was incredible. He handled it all with confidence, like he didn't care what anyone thought, as long as we were together."

"Wow," Lucy murmured. "That doesn't sound like the workaholic control freak you've been complaining about for six months."

"He's different," Devney said. "Or maybe he's the same, and I'm seeing more of him now. Parts he kept hidden before."

"The parts worth falling in love with," Lucy supplied, her usual snark replaced by genuine emotion.

"Yeah." Devney said. "Those parts."

They spent the next half-hour catching up—Lucy filling her in on bakery drama and a potential expansion to a second location, Devney sharing more details about the aftermath of their Martha's Vineyard revelations. The conversation flowed easily between them, punctuated by laughter and the random customer entering the bakery.

As Lucy began closing up shop, she flipped the sign to *Closed* and started counting the register. Devney helped wipe down tables and straighten chairs, falling back into the routine they'd established during countless evenings when she'd stop by after work.

"So," Lucy said, hanging up her apron as they finished the closing routine, "what's the plan with Ronan? Are you moving in together? Planning a real engagement? Adopting a cat named Spreadsheet?"

Devney choked on her last sip of tea. "We're taking it slow," she said once she'd recovered. "Well, slow-ish. He gave me a key to his place yesterday."

"A key?" Lucy's expression showed her surprise. "That's significant."

"I know. It has a little sunflower charm on the keychain."

"Oh my God," Lucy groaned, though her eyes were twinkling. "He's turning into a romantic. This is your doing, isn't it? You've corrupted him."

"Maybe a little," Devney conceded. "But he's still Ronan. He had a spreadsheet for our first date options."

They dissolved into laughter that was unrestrained, carrying with it a sense of release and repair, the kind that only best friends share. As they were recovering, the bell above the door chimed, drawing their attention.

Ronan stood in the doorway, looking simultaneously

imposing and out of place in his perfectly tailored suit. His gaze swept the bakery once before landing on Devney, the subtle shift in his eyes a little more open, a little less defended, still having the power to make her pulse race.

"Come on in," Lucy called from behind the counter. "We were expecting you." She glanced at her watch. "Six fifty-five. I'm impressed."

Ronan stepped into the bakery, closing the door behind him. He crossed to where Devney sat, leaning down to press a brief kiss to her temple before turning to face Lucy. "You must be Lucy," he said, extending his hand. "I've heard a great deal about you."

Lucy grasped his hand with a firm shake. "And I've heard volumes about you, Mr. Wilder. Some of it recently revised."

The corner of Ronan's mouth twitched. "Ronan, please."

"Ronan," Lucy amended, gesturing for him to sit. "Fair warning—I'm going to ask you extremely personal questions over dinner, and I expect honest answers."

"Lucy!" Devney said, shooting her friend a warning look.

"What?" Lucy shrugged, unrepentant. "He's dating my best friend. Standard best-friend protocols apply."

Ronan didn't seem bothered by Lucy's directness. If anything, he appeared amused. "I see your point," he said, his tone serious, though a new light danced in his eyes. "I'd expect nothing less from anyone who cares about Devney."

Lucy quickly covered her surprise and said, "Well, good. I made reservations at Vincenzo's for 7:15. We should head over now if we don't want to lose our table."

"I'll get my coat," Devney said, rising from her chair. As she passed Ronan, his fingers tightened around hers in a reassuring way.

"How was Tokyo?" she asked.

"Impatient," he replied with a slight shrug. "But manageable. Gabriel's handling the call follow-up."

"You delegated?" Devney asked, feigning shock. "Who are you, and what have you done with Ronan Wilder?"

That look surfaced again—the one that made her pulse skip and her thoughts scatter. "I'm learning to prioritize," he said, his low voice firm and unwavering. "Some things matter more than quarterly projections."

"I'm honored to rank above spreadsheets," she teased.

"You aren't on the same chart, Devney," he said, his voice dropping. "Spreadsheets are a tool to build a business. You are the reason the business is worth building."

"If you two can tear yourselves away from whatever intense thing you've got going on," Lucy interrupted from the door, coat and purse already in hand, "we have twelve minutes to make it across the street before they give away our table."

Dinner at the small Italian restaurant was a revelation. Devney had expected awkwardness, stilted conversation, perhaps even some minor disaster. Instead, she watched in amazement as Ronan and Lucy fell into an unexpected rhythm —her friend's blunt questions met with his progressively more open and candid answers.

"So," Lucy said, twirling pasta around her fork, "when did you realize you were in love with her and not playing a role?"

Devney choked on her wine. "Lucy!"

"When she made soup in my kitchen," Ronan answered. The simple admission silenced both women. He looked at Devney, vulnerability in his gaze. "I had a fever. You were in my kitchen making your grandmother's soup. It felt like home."

The restaurant around them seemed to fade away.

"That's—" Lucy began, then cleared her throat. "That's romantic."

"It wasn't meant to be," Ronan said, his eyes still on Devney. "It was the truth."

The rest of dinner passed in a blur of shared stories and

unexpected laughter. Ronan revealed glimpses of himself that Devney was still discovering—his dry humor emerging more frequently, his observations genuine rather than calculating. By the time they finished dessert, Lucy was looking at him with grudging approval.

"Well," she said as they stepped outside the restaurant into the cool evening air, "I have to admit, you're not what I expected, Ronan Wilder."

"Is that a compliment?" he asked.

"Let's call it an observation," Lucy said, her voice all mischief and zero apology. She turned to Devney and wrapped her in a quick hug. "Call me tomorrow," she whispered. "He'll do."

Devney laughed, hugging her back. "I'll take that as your official blessing."

As Lucy headed back toward the bakery, Ronan guided Devney to his car, his hand at her back offering firm, reassuring support.

They drove in easy silence for a few minutes, the city lights streaking past. The air outside had cooled, but the heat between them held.

"Your friend is formidable," Ronan said, as he turned onto her street.

"She likes you," Devney said, glancing over at him. "That's high praise from Lucy. She doesn't approve of anyone."

"I'm honored," he said, and she knew he meant it.

When they pulled up to her building, he turned off the engine but made no move to get out.

"Coming up?" she asked, her heart racing despite how natural the question felt.

"I was hoping you'd ask," he said. "Though I should mention, we've been making excellent use of my bed. Yours deserves some attention too."

She laughed, the sound bright in the quiet car. "Equal opportunity sleeping arrangements?"

"Something like that," he said, getting out and circling to open her door.

In the elevator, the tension was different than before, this time the confident anticipation of lovers who knew what awaited them.

"I love you," he said as she fumbled with her keys. "I should've said it on Martha's Vineyard. I'm saying it now."

"I love you too," she said, finally getting the door open. "All of you."

He followed her inside, and this time there was no hesitation, no pretense. Just them, real and together, with all the time in the world.

Chapter 25

THE NOVEMBER AIR carried a distinct chill as he surveyed the property from the dock of his lake house. Workers moved efficiently across the lawn, setting up the heated tent, arranging fire pits, installing heat lamps along the pathways. The forecast promised clear skies but temperatures dropping into the low forties by evening.

Behind him, the sound of car doors slamming announced Knox and Gabriel's arrival.

"Are you planning to help at all?" Knox called from the porch, a case of champagne balanced in his arms. "Or is manual labor beneath the great Ronan Wilder?"

He turned. "I'm making sure everything's set up correctly."

"It's a party to celebrate the Beauchamp deal," Gabriel said, crossing the lawn. "Not a state dinner. I think we can manage without your micromanagement."

"The first milestone deserves proper recognition," he replied, climbing the steps to join them. "The Beauchamps took a significant risk trusting us. This is the least I can do."

Knox set down the case with a satisfied grin. "A weekend at the lake house, open bar, and you're actually hosting instead of hiding in your office. Who are you and what have you done with Ronan Wilder?"

He ignored the jab. Three months ago, he would have delegated this entire event. But things had changed. He had changed.

"Where do you want the champagne?" Knox asked.

"Under the tent. There's a table set up near the bar."

Gabriel studied him. "You're unusually invested in this party."

"It's a significant milestone," he said evenly. "The Beauchamps deserve recognition for their trust in Oath Capital."

"And it has nothing to do with impressing a certain someone?" Knox asked.

"Devney will be here, yes. The Beauchamps are bringing her."

"How convenient," Gabriel said dryly.

He ignored the implication, checking his watch. Five o'clock. The staff would start arriving at five-thirty, the Beauchamps at six. Everything was on schedule.

Inside, they gathered in the great room, its wall of windows overlooking the lake. Knox popped open a bottle of champagne and poured three glasses.

"To the Beauchamp deal," Knox said, raising his glass. "And to Devney Sinclair, who managed the impossible."

"What's that?" Ronan accepted the glass.

"Making you tolerable to be around." Knox grinned. "You've been almost human lately. It's disturbing."

Gabriel raised his own glass. "To efficiency. And to whatever has you checking your phone every thirty seconds."

The three men clinked glasses. The champagne was bright and crisp against the afternoon chill.

"I don't want to miss a text from Devney," he admitted, checking his phone again.

"The office gossip mill has been in overdrive since you two went public," Knox said, sprawling in an armchair. "Martha's Vineyard changed you."

"I'm still focused on the business," he said.

"You bought her sunflowers," Gabriel pointed out. "You, who once called them 'chaotic and impractical.'"

"She likes them."

"Exactly." Gabriel's expression was unreadable. "You've changed."

The words struck deeper than intended. He'd spent months trying to prove he was different from the man who'd proposed a fake engagement—trying to show Devney through actions rather than words that his feelings were genuine.

"The Beauchamps will be here at six," he said, deflecting. "I should check on the catering."

"Running away from feelings?" Knox called after him. "That's the old Ronan. I thought we'd evolved past that."

He didn't respond, stepping out onto the porch where the workers were putting finishing touches on the tent. The heaters glowed with warmth, the fire pits were arranged in a perfect semicircle, and the bar gleamed with bottles and glassware.

His phone buzzed.

DEVNEY: Looking forward to tonight. The Beauchamps are bringing me with them. They said they want my opinion on something. See you there!

He smiled despite himself and typed back.

RONAN: Perfect. Dress warmly. It will be cold.

DEVNEY: Always so practical. See you soon. Love you.

> RONAN: Love you too.

He pocketed the phone and returned inside, where Knox and Gabriel were arguing about the optimal placement of heat lamps.

"You're overthinking it," Knox said.

"I'm thinking about it the correct amount," Gabriel countered. "Unlike some people who just throw money at problems and hope they resolve themselves."

"That's rich coming from you—"

"The heat lamps are fine," Ronan interrupted. "Focus on making sure the sound system works. I don't want anyone freezing in silence."

The afternoon progressed with increasing speed. The catering staff arrived and began setting up the bar and food stations. At five-thirty, the charter bus from Oath Capital pulled up, and employees began filing out, their faces bright with anticipation.

He greeted them from the porch, accepting thanks and congratulations on the Beauchamp deal.

Within minutes, the party was in full swing. Laughter and conversation filled the heated tent, fire pits crackled invitingly, and the November sky deepened to twilight.

He positioned himself near the entrance, checking his watch. 5:55.

Lucy arrived, making her way to the dessert display she'd provided. She caught his eye and smiled.

Just before six, headlights appeared at the top of the driveway.

His heart rate increased. Devney was here.

The car doors opened. Eleanor emerged first, elegant in a long coat. Then Andrew, offering his hand to Devney in the backseat.

And then she stepped out.

She wore a deep blue dress with a cream-colored cardigan, a cashmere scarf wrapped loosely around her neck. Her cheeks were flushed from the cold, her hair tumbling around her shoulders in soft waves.

She looked toward the tent, confusion crossing her face as she took in the crowd, the lights, the celebration.

Then her eyes found his.

For one suspended moment, everything else fell away—the noise of the party, the cold November air, the sixty people watching. There was only her.

Beautiful.

She started toward the tent, and he moved to meet her.

Showtime.

Chapter 26

THE LAKE HOUSE glowed with warmth as they stepped out of the car. Fire pits flickered across the lawn, heat lamps cast amber light across the heated tent, and the entire Oath Capital staff mingled with champagne glasses in hand.

Ronan appeared at the edge of the tent, his face lighting up when he saw her. He crossed the distance in quick strides.

"You made it." He kissed her cheek, then turned to Eleanor and Andrew. "Thank you for bringing her."

"Our pleasure," Eleanor said with a smile.

A server appeared with a tray of champagne. Ronan handed glasses to each of them, his fingers lingering on hers for just a moment.

"Come on," he said, guiding them inside the tent. "Everyone's here."

She stepped inside, taking in the crowd. Colleagues from the office, the catering staff moving efficiently, and—

"Lucy?" Her voice pitched higher. "What are you doing here?"

Lucy grinned from her spot near the dessert display.

"Ronan invited me to stay. Said I should enjoy the party after delivering the desserts."

Before she could process that, Ronan pulled a pen from his pocket and tapped it against his champagne glass. The sharp clink cut through the conversations. The tent quieted.

"Thank you all for coming tonight," he said, his voice carrying across the space. He turned to Eleanor and Andrew. "And a special thank you to the Beauchamps—for your trust in Oath Capital, for taking a chance on us, and for everything you've done to make this partnership a success."

Applause rippled through the crowd. Eleanor inclined her head graciously. Andrew gave Ronan a subtle nod, and Ronan winked back at them.

Then his gaze found Devney's, and something flickered in his eyes. A hint of nervousness.

She narrowed her eyes at him. "What are you up to?"

He set down his glass and took both her hands.

"You think you're here to celebrate the first milestone of the Beauchamp deal," he said, his voice wavering slightly. "And that's true."

He paused.

"But hopefully, it will be a different type of celebration than the one you're expecting."

His fingers trembled.

"I wanted everyone here tonight because I want the world to know how much I love Devney Sinclair. And I couldn't wait another minute to lock down the most important merger of my life."

Laughter rippled through the crowd.

"The first time I asked you to marry me, it was a charade. A business decision. This time, it's real."

He knelt.

Her hand flew to her mouth as he drew a velvet box from

his pocket. Around them, gasps. Lucy's sob cutting through the silence.

"You changed everything." His voice cracked. "You challenged me. Pushed me. Saw through every wall I built. You made me realize that success isn't measured in profit margins or market share. It's measured in moments like this—standing before the woman I love, terrified and hopeful and certain that you're the only future I want."

He opened the box, and for a heartbeat, she forgot to breathe.

Inside, a vivid yellow diamond sat nestled in a bed of velvet, its deep golden hue catching the amber light of the tent. Surrounding it, smaller white stones were set in a delicate, radiating pattern of petals. Her breath hitched as the shape came into focus. A sunflower. It was a sudden, sharp ache of recognition—the one flower that had always meant home.

"I love you," he said, his voice a low vibration that grounded her. "Will you marry me? For real this time?"

Tears spilled down her cheeks.

"Yes." Barely audible. Then louder, voice breaking, "Yes!"

He slid the ring onto her finger as cheers erupted around them. He rose, and she threw herself into his arms.

"I can't believe you did this."

She pulled back, looking at him. "Is this why the Beauchamps insisted on bringing me tonight?"

He nodded. "They knew. And Lucy. Everyone else thought this was just a Beauchamp deal celebration."

"You orchestrated all of this? A fake property viewing, a surprise party, witnesses—"

"I wanted it to be perfect. You deserve perfect."

Lucy crashed into them both. "Oh my God, Dev! Look at that ring!"

She lifted her hand, and the yellow diamond caught the firelight.

"You always remembered." She met his eyes over Lucy's shoulder. "The sunflowers."

"I remember everything about you."

For a moment, they just looked at each other, the noise of the celebration fading into the background. Then Lucy tugged on her arm, demanding to see the ring again, and the moment broke.

The rest of the evening passed in champagne toasts and congratulations. Eleanor and Andrew appeared with warm smiles. Knox regaled anyone who would listen with increasingly embellished tales about their courtship. Gabriel stood slightly apart, observing. Through it all, Ronan stayed at her side, his hand finding hers repeatedly.

Later, they escaped to the dock under the pretense of getting air.

He wrapped his arms around her from behind as they stared out at the dark water.

"You really thought I might say no?"

"I hoped you wouldn't." He pressed his chin against her hair. "But hope and certainty are different things."

She leaned back against him. "I'm certain. About you. About us. About all of it."

"Good." He pressed a kiss to her temple. "Because I'm not letting you change your mind now. I have witnesses."

She laughed and turned in his arms. Fire pits flickered behind them. She reached up and traced the line of his jaw.

"For the record, this was much better than the first proposal."

"The bar was fairly low. The last time you bought your own ring."

"You've improved your technique. But you know what the best part was?"

"What?"

"You were scared." She touched his chest, right over his

heart. "You let everyone see it. The real you, not the CEO mask. That's what made it perfect."

His hand covered hers. "You've made me brave. Or maybe foolish. I'm not sure there's a difference anymore."

"Definitely foolish. But I'll take it."

They stayed there until Knox called them back. Until the cold became impossible to ignore. Until duty demanded they rejoin their own engagement party.

Chapter 27
SIX MONTHS LATER

THE MIRROR in Eleanor's guest suite didn't lie. She looked like an actual bride in a dress that made her heart skip when she first tried it on. Simple, elegant ivory with delicate lace sleeves that made her feel both beautiful and like herself. Six months after his lakeside proposal, here they were on Martha's Vineyard, about to make it official.

"If you touch your hair one more time, I swear I'll stab you with this bobby pin," Lucy threatened, brandishing her weapon of choice. "I've spent forty minutes getting these curls right."

"Sorry," she mumbled, dropping her hands to her sides. "Nervous habit."

"Nervous? You?" Lucy stepped back, assessing her handiwork with a critical eye. "The woman who told off an entire office full of people and then flew across the sound on a ferry to fix it? Puh-lease."

She laughed despite the butterflies in her stomach. "That was different. This is forever."

"Forever with a guy who looks at you like you're the only

star in his sky." Lucy tucked a final pin into her updo. "Do you know how rare that is? Most women would kill for that look."

"That's dramatic, even for you," she laughed.

"I'm serious!" Lucy insisted, turning Devney to face her. "I've never seen a man more in love. It's actually sickening how perfect you two are together. Makes me want to hurl glitter all over your disgustingly happy life."

She shook her head, smiling. "You have such a way with words."

"It's my gift," she shrugged, then reached for the diamond earrings. "These were your grandmother's, right?"

She nodded, emotion clogging her throat. "I wish she could have been here."

"She is," Lucy said, all humor dropping from her voice as she squeezed her friend's hand. "She'd be so proud of you, Dev. Finding genuine love in the middle of a fake engagement. That's some serious rom-com material."

"We should sell the rights," she joked, blinking back tears. "That might fund your bakery expansion."

"Don't tempt me," Lucy grinned, then pointed sternly at her eyes. "And don't you dare cry. I spent too long on your makeup."

A knock interrupted them. Eleanor Beauchamp entered, elegant in a silver-blue dress that complemented her hair. Her eyes widened when she saw the bride.

"Oh, my dear," she breathed, pressing a hand to her heart. "You look beautiful."

"Thank you." Her voice wavered. "And thank you for all of this. The estate, the dress…everything."

Eleanor waved away her thanks. "It's been our pleasure. Andrew and I haven't enjoyed ourselves this much in years."

"Still," she insisted, "you've gone from business associates to…I don't even know what to call it."

"Family," Eleanor said. "You've become family to us, and we're so happy to share in this day with you."

"She's probably been planning your wedding since Martha's Vineyard," Lucy said. "Face it, you've been adopted."

She elbowed her friend discreetly but couldn't deny the truth in her words. Eleanor had taken her under her wing with surprising grace, the kind that paid no mind to social standing.

"Speaking of planning," Eleanor continued, "it's nearly time. Ronan is waiting, and if his pacing wears a hole in our lawn, Andrew will never let him hear the end of it."

She laughed at the image of her usually composed fiancé wearing a path in the grass. "We can't have that."

Lucy handed her a bouquet—a simple mix of cream roses, greenery, and one cheerful yellow sunflower nestled in the center.

"Ready to get hitched to Mr. Wilder?"

"More than ready."

Lucy smoothed the lace at her wrists and gave her a look that was one blink away from misty. "He's going to lose it when he sees you."

Devney laughed, nerves shifting low in her stomach. "No promises."

The doors opened, and Andrew Beauchamp stepped forward, extending his arm with the calm certainty of one used to leading.

She slipped her hand through the crook, then hesitated. "Thank you." Her voice was soft. "For stepping into this role. For being—" her voice caught, "—what I didn't have."

A gentle, fatherly look replaced his previous more reserved expression. "Happy to fill in as the father of the bride," he said. "Even happier it's you."

And then the music began. Bach's "Cello Suite No. 1 in G Major."

It floated through the garden, delicate and rich, the notes curling around her like a memory. She had chosen it herself. Not because it was traditional, but because it mattered. Because months ago, right here on this estate, she'd talked Ronan into playing it before a cocktail party. He'd resisted. She'd pushed. And when he finally gave in, the sound of that cello had undone her. It was the first time she saw past the armor. The first time she knew there was more to him than strategy and steel. Now, walking toward him to that same piece, the significance of the moment settled over her—full, radiant, and real.

The path curved through the garden, sunlight heating the stone beneath her steps. The rows of white chairs blurred at the edges. The murmur of the guests faded.

At the far end stood the arbor. Simple. Beautiful. Framed in white drapery and green vines, it looked like a scene from a dream. Her breath caught when she saw them—sunflowers, tucked into the arrangement.

Just a few. Just enough. Her throat tightened. And then she saw him.

Ronan was beneath the arbor, impeccably dressed, his posture resolute, though his features betrayed the powerful, barely contained emotions within him. He looked at her like he couldn't believe she was real.

Each step pulled her closer. When they reached the front, Andrew gently placed her hand into Ronan's. "She's yours now," he said. "Take care of her."

"I will." Ronan's gaze locked on hers. She handed off her bouquet, adjusted her grip on his hands, and felt everything inside her settle.

Then he reached into his pocket and pulled out a small card. "I had this all planned out," he said, his voice low but sure. "A perfectly crafted speech with exactly the right words to express what you mean to me."

He glanced down at the card, then back to her, regret in his expression. "But I realize now that's not what matters."

To everyone's astonishment, including hers, he tucked the card back into his pocket. "I don't need a script with you, Devney. You've taught me that the best moments in life are the unplanned ones. The ones where we allow ourselves to feel."

Someone seated nearby let out a sigh. Ronan Wilder, embracing spontaneity? The world had tilted on its axis.

"I love you," he continued. "Not because it makes sense on paper, but because you make me laugh when I least expect it. Because you see the man I am, not the man everyone thinks I am. Because when I'm with you, I'm better than I ever thought I could be."

He took a deep breath. "I promise to love you honestly and completely. To value your happiness as my own. To build a life with you that's rich in laughter and adventure. And I promise to always let you have the last word in at least twenty percent of our arguments—which is far more generous than my initial offer."

That earned a genuine laugh from her and their guests. She blinked back tears, overwhelmed by his raw honesty. When it was her turn, she drew a deep breath, composing herself before she spoke.

"Ronan," she began, her voice wobbling. "If anyone had told me a year ago that I'd be standing here today, I would have laughed in their face. Not because I couldn't imagine loving you—that part happened without me noticing—but because I couldn't imagine you loving me back.

"We started with a fake engagement and ended up with a real one. Talk about a plot twist."

That earned another laugh from their guests, and his lips curved in that quiet expression she'd grown to cherish—just shy of a smile.

"I promise to keep challenging you," she continued. "To

never let you retreat behind that stoic CEO mask when what you need is to be seen. I promise to be your partner in every sense—supporting your dreams while pursuing my own."

She squeezed his hands. "And I promise to love you through every version of yourself—the serious CEO, the one who plays cello when he thinks no one is listening, and all the new versions we haven't met yet. I even promise to pretend I don't notice when you organize the refrigerator by expiration date, even though we both know I'll mess it up within twenty-four hours."

By the time they exchanged rings, she couldn't have stopped her expression of joy if she tried. When the officiant pronounced them husband and wife, his kiss was both tender and possessive, a public declaration of private feelings that made her heart race.

The reception flowed seamlessly onto the terrace overlooking the ocean, the setting sun casting light across tables draped in white linen. She floated from group to group, accepting congratulations, laughing at Knox's increasingly outrageous toasts, and always, always finding her husband's eyes across the room.

"If anyone had told me six months ago that I'd see Ronan Wilder glowing this much, I would have checked them for a fever," Knox said, appearing at her side with two champagne flutes.

She accepted the offered glass. "Get used to it. I plan to make him laugh more than he thinks he's capable of."

"Good." He clinked his glass against hers. "He deserves it. And so do you, Sunshine."

With the reception in full swing—guests mingling, laughter rising, the sky sliding toward dusk—she stepped away, just long enough to steady herself and take it all in. The edge of the terrace offered a view of the water still kissed with light, and was a secluded spot away from the buzz of celebration.

She was still absorbing it when arms slid around her waist. "Escaping already?" Ronan murmured in her ear.

She leaned back against him. "I'm taking a moment. It's been quite a day."

"Any regrets?" His voice held that particular tender inflection she knew so well, reserved only for their private moments.

She turned to face him. "Not a single one. You?"

"Only that it took me so long to realize what had been there all along." An odd sight over his shoulder caught her eye —a server weaving through the crowd, her hair pulled into a severe bun. But it wasn't her pace that caught Devney's attention.

It was her stare. Fixed. Sharp. Directed straight at Gabriel, who stood near the bar mid-laugh.

"What is it?" Ronan asked, noticing her shift.

"That server," she murmured. "She hasn't looked away from Gabriel."

They watched as the woman crossed the terrace, her steps quickening. She carried a tray of champagne flutes, the glasses catching the fading light. As she reached the bar, she stopped abruptly.

The tray tilted.

Everything seemed to slow. The champagne flutes slid forward, crystal catching the last rays of sunset as they tumbled through the air. Then they hit the stone terrace—one, two, three sharp cracks followed by the musical shatter of glass. Champagne spread across the stone in a golden pool, bubbles fizzing against the terracotta.

Other servers rushed forward with towels and a dustpan, but the woman didn't move. She just stared at Gabriel.

"Tessa," Gabriel said, and she could hear the shock in his voice.

The woman took a step back. "I never thought I'd see you

again." Then she turned and ran. Across the terrace. Through the archway. Gone.

She stared after her. "What just happened?"

"I don't know," Ronan said, his eyes on Gabriel. "But he does."

She opened her mouth to ask another question, but Eleanor appeared at her side, graceful and unshaken. "It's time for the first dance."

Ronan took her hand. As he led her toward the center of the terrace, Devney looked back one last time.

Gabriel hadn't moved. He stood there, glass in hand, watching the space where the server Tessa had vanished—frozen, like his past had just crashed into his present and he hadn't figured out what to do about it yet.

"Should we be worried?" she asked.

"Tomorrow," Ronan said, pulling her close as the music began. "Tonight is ours."

As they moved together on the floor, the world narrowed to them—to the pressure of his hand at her waist, his breath against her hair, the constant, strong beat of his heart under her hand, grounding her.

"I love you, Mrs. Wilder," he whispered.

"I love you, too." She smiled against his chest. "No strategy required."

The celebration carried on around them—music swelling, glasses clinking, laughter floating from the terrace—but they stayed in their own orbit. He reached for her hand, their fingers finding each other with instinctive ease.

"Happy?" he asked, the single word carrying everything he couldn't say.

She leaned into him. "Completely."

And for a long moment, she held on.

To the man she had once pretended to love.

The one who now held her heart without question.

What lived between them was no longer a lie. It was real. It was claimed. It was earned.

Somewhere between the pretending and the truth, between resistance and surrender, she had done the one thing she never meant to do. She had stayed long enough to matter. She had pressed where it hurt. She had refused to let him remain untouched.

She had changed him.

She had conquered him.

She had tamed him.

Next:

Gabriel in *Trusting Mr. Sterling*

Also by Kelly Collins

The Billionaire Hearts Club

Taming Mr. Wilder

Trusting Mr. Sterling

About the Author

Kelly Collins is a bestselling, award-winning author of feel-good small-town romance filled with heart, heat, and happily-ever-afters. Her books are perfect for readers who crave heartwarming contemporary love stories, sassy heroines, and slow-burn romances with cinnamon roll heroes you'll wish were real.

With humor, charm, and emotional depth, Kelly brings to life tight-knit towns, unforgettable characters, and the kind of love that feels like coming home. When she's not plotting her next happily-ever-after, she's sipping strong coffee and dreaming up heroes who are tough on the outside and gooey in the middle.

Come for the charm, stay for the swoon—and don't be surprised if you fall in love with the whole town.

A small press bound by the belief that every voice matters.

Sign up for our newsletter to learn about new releases and more.
https://oliver-heberbooks.com/subscribe/

Follow us on social media:

facebook.com/oliverheberbooks

instagram.com/oliverheberbooks

amazon.com/oliverheberbooks

youtube.com/@OliverHeberBooksPublisher